To Gary and
with lots of l.
enjoy the stories.
Anne Digman Nov 2022

FROM THE
BURGH
AND BEYOND

Burgh Blatherers

PREFACE

The Burgh Blatherers is an Edinburgh based group with a relatively short but vibrant history. We started as a small group of like minded friends coming together informally to practise and share stories in a safe and supportive environment. These mutually supportive gatherings were given a sense of focus and direction when dynamic storyteller, Calum Lykan launched a series of successful "Open Mic" sessions upstairs at Edinburgh's Waverley Bar, a venue with a long and continuing reputation for supporting the traditional arts. Members of the original group were quick to attend these early sessions and shortly afterwards the name "Burgh Blatherers" was first mooted and adopted.

It quickly became apparent that Burgh Blatherers seemed to meet a previously unrecognised need in an emerging storytelling community and numbers attending began to increase. The group relocated to the then Circus café across the road and Calum was to move to Canada and embark on a meteoric career as a Storyteller, Tour Guide and Master of Ceremonies.

Since by May 2016 the group had become established and was considering expanding their activities by embarking on their first public performance, the time seemed ripe to formalise their existence, adopt a constitution and open a bank account.

At this point the aims of the club were listed as: (a) to encourage and develop the skills of emergent and established storytellers. (b) to assist in organising, managing, and promoting storytelling programmes and events, and (c) to co-operate with sister organisations, local authorities, community groups and local cultural, artistic and educational organisations to promote storytelling.

Membership of the group increased through word of mouth. New members brought new ideas and skills and gradually the activities of the club have expanded. We regularly promote storytelling performances throughout the year with our popular "Winter Warmer" event held annually at the Scottish Storytelling Centre on or close to December 6th having established itself as a favourite curtain raiser for the festivities that await just round the corner.

Club members continue to participate fully in the wider storytelling world by supporting and mentoring those on the Apprenticeship Scheme, working on the committee of the Storytelling Forum and participating in Festivals and events throughout the UK. We are becoming an ever more recognisable player in the wider storytelling circle.

When, in March 2020, the country was plunged into lockdown as a result of the covid-19 pandemic, Burgh Blatherers and its members suffered along with the rest of the nation. Club meetings, planned performances, and all face-to-face contacts were banned for an indefinite period and the way ahead was unclear. Ramifications were mixed as some members embraced the whole "Zoom" culture with varying levels of expertise and enthusiasm. While some members preferred to wait until face-to-face meetings were reintroduced, for others a whole new world of opportunities was beginning to open up.

Our meetings, by necessity previously confined to those able to travel to Edinburgh, were now being accessed on Zoom by new-found friends from across the globe. As covid-19 restrictions start to recede in the memory it sometimes feels as if we have unwittingly found ourselves at the birth of a new art form. Whatever the future holds with regards to our live meetings our Zoom meetings will continue indefinitely in some form as we simultaneously demonstrate that we are "aa Jock Tamson's bairns" and that it is indeed "a small world".

Whether live or on Zoom Burgh Blatherers and its current membership strive to be true to its earliest objectives of providing a safe and supportive space where stories can be told, practised, and improved on and where feedback can be sought in a purely constructive spirit.

We like to think that our ethos and values are reflected in the shows that we continue to perform on a very regular basis that include the full variety of stories from the oral tradition, whether personal recollection, historical, self-penned or folk and traditional.

We have reproduced just such a "show" within the pages of "From the Burgh and Beyond", our members' first joint venture into print and our modest contribution to Scotland's "Year of Stories".

Bob Mitchell Chair 2022

WITH THANKS

We would like to thank all our fellow Blathering members included within these pages or not whose enthusiasm and support bring joy and community to all our storytelling.

Thanks also to

- The Book Whisperers, our inestimable publishers

- Donald Smith and all at The Scottish Storytelling Centre in Edinburgh

- Our editorial team: Bob Mitchell; Harriet Grindley; Maria MacDonell and Ruaridh Mackintosh

- Our Master of Ceremonies written and performed by Bob Mitchell.

- our Outside Eye envisaged and written by Maria MacDonell.

RUNNING ORDER

Here we are. Here we are at the Scottish Storytelling Centre in the heart of Edinburgh. Step inside. Welcome. Let's wait here in the Haggis Box Cafe before we go into the show.

Drink? Of course. And there's still time for food. Have you tried the haggis? It's amazing. And have you ever seen walls so green, furniture so finely fashioned? In a tale perhaps, a dream.

Who's here? Let's say hello. There are familiar faces and new, grey hair, brown hair, pink and fair. There are walking sticks and stilettos, dancing shoes and boots. Everyone is here. Everyone is here for our live lively story performance.

Some of us tellers are Edinburgh born and bred. Some have come here from far beyond. All of us love this place with its ever-changing skies, its surprises and delights, its shadows and light. We have traced our hands along its stones, felt the cobbles beneath our feet, filled our hearts with its history, marvelled at its sudden views. And we have stood many a time on Arthur's Seat with our faces to the wind and our gaze in all directions. For Edinburgh, this international city, welcomes everyone, reaching out across the world from the burgh and beyond.

So, fàilte, willkommen, वेलकम, welcome. Step inside.

Do you come with expectations? Will you be entertained and delighted? Will you laugh and will you cry? Will you fill with sorrow, or surprise? Will you travel far?

Listen.

1

Hearts are quickening, minds are calming, chatter is hushing. The door is open! And there's the announcement:

"Ladies and gentlemen. Please takes your seats for this evening's performance of From the Burgh and Beyond."

Ha Ha! Come on in. Bring your drink. Find a seat.

My, what a beautiful wooden room. It reaches as high as the sky. It is bubbling full of stories. Can you hear them whispering? They travel in many tongues. They have a sweet scent, sharp at times, old and young all at once, always moving, ever fresh.

Beyond the long window, out in the city, tall trees are waving in the breeze.

It's time. We are ready. Let's begin.

And who is this? It's Bob!

MASTER OF CEREMONIES

Bob Mitchell

Good evening, and a huge welcome to one and all. Thank you for coming. My name is Bob Mitchell, we are Burgh Blatherers and this is *From the Burgh and Beyond*.

Yes, my name is Bob Mitchell, and I am your host or MC for the evening or if you prefer, I am both your Ant and your Dec, lacking as I do the gravitas of a Bamber Gascoigne or a David Attenborough. My job, indeed my pleasure, is to introduce a whole potpourri of my fellow members of Burgh Blatherers and their wide-ranging variety of tales, some old, some new, some borrowed (and thus acknowledged) but fear not, I think that we have managed to steer clear of 'blue'.

The performance tonight will, as is our norm, be one of two halves with a short interval in the middle where you can avail yourselves of all that the Haggis Box has to offer, but now let me introduce you to the first of our very own offerings.

Franziska Droll first learned to love the stories from her father - as he from his father - in her native Black Forest, which is fascinating, but she has also called her infant daughter 'Heather' which I think is fabulous. You certainly don't have to go beyond our lovely burgh to see Scottish heather which is one of my very favourite species of plant.

Over to you, Franzi!

FRANZISKA DROLL

Originally from the Black Forest Franziska grew up surrounded by the tales of the Brothers Grimm and her father's funny anecdotes. She studied event management and became a tour guide, operating tours from Edinburgh and all around Scotland. This is when she learned and shared Scotland's rich storytelling culture. With the aim to make history fun and engaging, she embarked on her own storytelling journey. One night she stumbled over the Burgh Blatherers blathering in the pub and continues to enjoy the camaraderie and joy this group shared so generously with her.

THE THREE SKULLS

Franziska Droll

This tale has many origins and has travelled, as do all good stories, all around the world. Each version comes with its own twist and this is mine.

In the 1500s, Mary Stuart reigned over Scotland. But being a woman and the Queen of Scotland, wasn't the fairytale you might imagine, and it was *so* different from in France where she had also been Queen until the death of her husband in 1560. From the moment she arrived back at Leith to assert her right to the throne, the young widow was shown little welcome. And when she finally took up residence in Holyrood Palace, renowned woman hater and religious zealot John Knox proved her fiercest critic, demanding all sorts of things in the name of the people and church.

Fair to say – Mary and John didn't get on. They argued day in, day out.

One day John Knox arrived in the palace. He was just going to start yet another debate about God, when Mary raised her hand to silence him and said,

"Oh please Mr. Knox, not today. I am trying to solve this riddle that one of my courtiers has given me. For the life of me, I can't figure out the answer."

"Of course you can't," he replied with an arrogance only men in power possess. "You are only a woman! And therefore your mind is not capable of solving such complicated matters as riddles!"

Mary just waved his words aside, like you would a nasty fly, and continued thinking.

After a few moments of silence Knox asked, "What is it then? This *unsolvable* riddle?"

"Well," said Mary, "Here I have three seemingly identical skulls. Of course, they are not in fact identical, and the task is to figure out who they were, when they were alive."

And with this they began a fearsome debate, to try and solve the puzzle. They held the skulls up to the light. They touched them from all sides and looked at them from different angles, while the courtier who gave this challenge stayed in the background and simply shook his head, with each incorrect guess.

After hours and hours of guessing Mary and John finally gave up. And for the very first time in their lives, they agreed on one thing: this riddle was unsolvable - absolutely impossible in fact!

The courtier stepped forward and took the first skull in his hand. Out of his pocket he took a small piece of string and put it into the ear of the skull. The string went further and further into the skull until it disappeared completely.

"This skull belonged to a scholar", he said. "Everything he heard went in and was retained inside."

Next, he took the second skull and again put the string through the ear. This time the string reappeared on the other side of his head.

"This person was a fool. All the information he ever heard went straight out of his head again."

John Knox and Mary Queen of Scots leaned forward. They had nodded as they heard the explanations and they were excited to hear who the last skull belonged to.

The courtier held the last skull in his hand and placed a string through the ear. This time the string went inside and came out of the mouth. But now the string had a small twist in it.

"This one was the head of a storyteller. He listened to everything and retold what he learned. But he always put a little twist in it, for every storyteller makes a story his own."

John and Mary smiled. And for a few moments, they were able to forget their quarrels and enjoy the courtier's tale.

RUARIDH MACKINTOSH

Born and bred in Inverness, the capital of the Highlands, Ruaridh left to go to University in Glasgow to study physics and astronomy. He has since lived and worked in France, the Middle East and back in Scotland as a teacher, network engineer and tourist guide where he enjoys sharing stories of his native Highlands and his adopted city of Edinburgh.

CITY OF CONTRASTS

Ruaridh Mackintosh

Edinburgh has always been a city of contrasts: of hills and valleys, the old town and the new town, of enlightenment and of depravity. And there is no greater example of Edinburgh's depravity than in the year 1828.

To understand how these heinous events came to pass we need to go back to the 18th century when Scotland led the world in the Age of Enlightenment. Adam Smith, buried in the Canongate, became the father of economics and James Hutton, buried in Greyfriars', the father of geology. Then in 1771 one of the greatest intellectual achievements of the enlightenment was created here in Edinburgh: the monumental Encyclopaedia Britannica. (Which should really be the Encyclopaedia Scotica.)

Now in particular, Edinburgh University had a renowned medical school and in 1847, Professor James Young Simpson discovered something for which Queen Victoria herself was immensely grateful. After enduring seven excruciatingly painful childbirths with no anaesthetic, her last two children were delivered in the comparative comfort of being under the influence of chloroform. Out of personal gratitude Victoria made James Young Simpson Sir James Young Simpson.

But prior to chloroform, not just childbirth but all surgery was performed without anaesthetic. The technique was simple. First strap your patient securely to the operating table. Then take your scalpel or saw and as quickly as possible cut out the infected area or saw off the infected limb, trying your best to ignore the screams and spasms of your unfortunate patient. Speed was of the essence and one eminent Edinburgh professor of surgery Robert Liston (1794-1847) was known as "the fastest knife in the west end". He claimed he could amputate a leg in two and a half minutes and an arm in twenty-eight seconds. He performed live operations in front of his students who recorded his cases such as when he amputated a leg in two and a half minutes, but in his enthusiasm also amputated the patient's testicles. Or his most notorious case when he amputated the leg in under two and a half minutes, though the patient later died from gangrene. However, in his haste he also severed the fingers of his young assistant who likewise died from gangrene. But on top of that he slashed through the coat tails of a spectator, who got such a shock he dropped dead from a heart attack. It's thought to be the only operation in history with a three hundred percent mortality.

Now these were some of the cases of one of the most skilled and respected surgeons in the land. One dreads to think what the less skilled surgeons were like.

Surgeons desperately needed more knowledge and more practice. But the only way to gain this was by cutting people up and having a good look around. And there wasn't a long queue of volunteers for this. What was needed were people who did not mind being cut up, people who didn't wriggle around and scream. What was needed were dead people and lots of them.

And this gap in the market was filled by the resurrectionists, the body snatchers, who would break into a cemetery at night and quite literally raise the dead. They would look for a fresh grave, as smelly, decaying corpses were no use for dissecting and, using specially made wooden spades to avoid metal clinking against stone, would dig a hole only at the head of the grave, lower down a hook and snap off the end of the coffin lid. The head would then be lassoed, and the body pulled along the coffin, round the corner and up through the hole. It was stripped naked, (as stealing the clothes was a crime but stealing the body technically was not as it had no legal owner), then bundled into a sack and hoisted over the cemetery walls before being whisked off to the university medical school to be sold to the grateful professors for a very generous £8-£10.

Now, when such stories emerged, the good people of Edinburgh were outraged and graveyard walls were raised, mort safes designed to cage in fresh corpses and night watch towers built with armed guards to prevent the escape of the dead.

Then in 1828 along came two enterprising Irishmen who discovered an altogether easier way of obtaining dead bodies. William Burke and William Hare boarded in the Grassmarket. Hare married their landlady, then Burke's mistress moved in too. But they were not to all live happily ever after.

To be fair they had not set out to be mass murderers. It just kind of happened upon them. And their first victim was not even really their victim. Old Donald was an army pensioner staying at their lodgings who one day rather inconveniently died in his bed. Inconveniently because he owed them several weeks rent. However, they'd heard that good money could be had by supplying fresh corpses to the university so they bundled old Donald into a hand cart and wheeled him up to the school of anatomy where they sold Donald to an assistant of the renowned anatomy lecturer Dr Robert Knox for a very respectable £7 10s. Making money had never been so easy!

And when the money ran out, they waited, hoping someone else would conveniently die in their lodgings but alas no one did. So, when one of their tenants, a miller called Joseph fell ill, they thought they would give him a helping hand. They plied him with whisky, then sat on him and smothered him with his own pillow. This would become their standard modus operandi. It is quiet, efficient, leaves no tell-tale signs of murder and is still known to this day amongst the criminal fraternity as burking. Now there was plenty of low life in Edinburgh who had perhaps recently come to the city looking for work, no one knew them, and no one would miss them. And they were very grateful when the friendly Irishmen invited them back for a drink, offering free accommodation. And thus, in ten months they had notched up no less than 16 murders, with Dr Knox each time ensuring they were well recompensed for their efforts.

Some were old, some were young, some were beautiful. Such as Mary an eighteen-year-old *fille de joie* whom Knox was so taken with that he kept her naked body on display in his lab preserved in alcohol for three months before dissecting her. It's said a student recognised Mary. He'd been her client, but he kept quiet. Some were disabled, such as daft Jamie a likable lame boy, well known on the streets of Edinburgh. As Knox dissected him some students cried out that it was daft Jamie but Knox denied it and quickly amputated his head and feet.

And so it may have continued if it were not for the unexpected fortitude of Mrs Docherty, an elderly Irish lady, well known to enjoy a tipple. As usual they invited her to their lodgings and plied her with drink but mid-burking she managed to scream loud enough to alert the neighbours, but alas too late to save herself. By the time the police arrived the body was already gone but they managed to trace it … to Dr. Knox's dissecting rooms.

The case was not, however, clear cut, as other than Mrs Doherty, the rest of the evidence had been cut to pieces and conveniently disposed of by Dr Knox. To secure a conviction Hare was offered immunity for turning King's witness. Thus, on Christmas eve 1828 William Burke and his mistress Helen McDougal went on trial for the murders and just twenty-four hours later, on Christmas morning, the jury delivered their verdicts; for McDougal not proven, for Burke, guilty.

And on 28 January in the Lawn Market, in front of a jeering crowd of twenty-five thousand William Burke swung from the gallows. Window-seats in tenements overlooking the scaffold were hired out at prices from five shillings to £1.

But that was not quite the end of William Burke because the next day following the judge's orders, Burke's body was taken to the university anatomy school and in front of a packed lecture theatre was publicly dissected; not by Dr Knox, but by

13

his colleague Professor Munro who dipped his quill in Burke's blood and wrote,

"This is written in the blood of murderer William Burke. The blood is from his head".

Now I know what you are all thinking. If only you too could have been there to behold that butchered body, to view these villainous vertebrae, to contemplate that contemptible cranium.

But you can be there. Because the sordid skeleton of William Burke is to this day on display in the University Anatomy Museum and in Surgeon's Hall you can view a book, the leather cover of which is made from …yes, it's made from the tanned skin of William Burke.

And the events of 1828 are immortalised by generations of Edinburgh children chanting:

Up the close and down the stair,
In the house with Burke and Hare.
Burke's the butcher, Hare's the thief,
Knox, the boy who buys the beef.

BEVERLEY CASEBOW

Beverley was born and brought up in south London, but a family holiday inspired a lifelong love of Scotland where she has now lived for more than 30 years. She has spent most of her career working in and around the Royal Mile, in Edinburgh City Museums and the National Library of Scotland, where her passion for Scottish culture, history, and stories has been nurtured. It was a natural transition from this into the world of traditional storytelling, nourished by the warm, supportive community at the Scottish Storytelling Centre. She enjoys stories rooted in the natural world, with a touch of magic and enchantment.

THE SECRET COMMONWEALTH

Beverley Casebow

As someone who's worked in museums and libraries, I'm interested in folktales and stories that have a link with material culture. Robert Kirk's notebooks are in the National Library of Scotland, where I work, and I feel a particular connection with the Reverend and his story. Whilst researching this story, I visited Aberfoyle and walked to the tree where some say Robert Kirk still resides in the fairy realm. As I was standing there, a high branch snapped off for no apparent reason, fell, and narrowly missed my head! Like this story, it seemed to be a warning that we should always respect the wee folk and take care not to upset them. I hope they won't mind this story appearing in the book!

On the first day of May 1641, in the Gaelic-speaking parish of Aberfoyle, the Minister's wife gave birth to a son. He was the seventh of seven sons, and his parents christened him Robert.

Already, the tongues of the *bodachs* and *cailleachs*, the old men and women of the place, were busy.

"Och, the seventh son!" said one old *cailleach*.

"Aye, and born on the first of May too," replied a *bodach*, "the time when the veil between our world and the other world is thin."

For at that time, in the Highlands and Islands, and across the sea in Ireland, the belief was strong that the seventh son had the vision to see through the veil to other worlds, and through time, into the future.

And even before he reached the age of seven, young Robert seemed to be gifted with the sight of things to come. For hadn't he told how wee Mairi McGregor would be taken by the *each uisge*, the water horse, only two days before she was found, drowned and dead by the edge of the loch? And the boy had an uncanny look about him, and spent too many hours alone on Doon Hill, the hill of the *sidhe*, there behind the manse; it seemed to draw him like a magnet.

Robert also loved to spend time with old Morag, listening to her stories of kelpies, and brownies, and his favourite, the hidden folk, the *sidhe*, the fairy folk.

One day, looking into the boy's eyes, she said,

"Some bairns, Robbie, are taken by the fairy folk, away into the fairy hill, and in the cradle a fairy child is left in their likeness, in their likeness, Robbie."

"And who are the fairies?" asked Robert, wide-eyed.

"They are the between folk," said Morag, "neither human folk nor angels; they have their own ways. They are hidden, but at times, between the darkness and the light, between the changing of the seasons, they can be seen by those who know how to look, by those with the gift of sight, Robbie."

It was from his father, the Minister, that Robert heard the great stories from the Bible: Jonah in the belly of the giant whale; the miracle of Christ raising Lazarus from the dead; Moses parting the Red Sea by raising his staff; and Christ himself rising from the tomb on the third day. These stories, whether from old Morag or from his father, fascinated Robert.

And, with his father's help and encouragement, he would study the Good Book, in English and Latin, for there was as yet no translation of the Bible in Gaelic, the tongue he knew best. He worked hard at his studies, grew into a fine scholar and at last he journeyed to the great city of Edinburgh to study Divinity at New College, and to follow his father into the Ministry.

Aged twenty, and fresh from university, he took up his first post as Minister at Balquhidder, Stirlingshire. When not tending to the needs of his parishioners, he could be seen in the gloaming, wandering over the fields, and to nearby Ben

Sidhean, and studying far into the night, working on Gaelic translations of the Bible, and the Scottish metrical psalms.

After the death of his father, Robert moved back to his childhood home of Aberfoyle, to look after the parish there. And ever was he seen, by the moonlight, on the slopes of his childhood haunt, Doon Hill, the hill of the *sidhe*.

He would still spend many hours with Morag, now an old, old lady, and she would say,

"Take care, Robbie, take care. You don't want to come too close or be meddling too deep with the folk of the other world. There's a danger in it, Robbie. Mind what I say now."

The Episcopalian Bishop, hearing rumours of Robert's nocturnal wanderings, and of his talk of the fairy folk, also warned him against encouraging "pagan superstitions amongst his parishioners."

But like Hamlet, Robert couldn't help but believe that "there are more things in heaven and earth than are dreamt of in our philosophy." So great was his fascination with the supernatural and for worlds beyond the veil, that he began gathering accounts from his parishioners, together with his own encounters with the other world, into a manuscript, which he called "The Secret Commonwealth, a scholarly treatise on the hidden ways of elves, fauns, and fairies."

Not long after he had finished this, but before he had found a publisher, Robert Kirk's body was found one evening at dusk, on the slopes of Doon Hill, the fairy hill. At his burial, standing by the grave, old Morag muttered,

"I warned ye Robbie, not to meddle. The wee folk have surely taken you for telling their secret ways."

Only a few days after the burial, Robert Kirk appeared in spirit form before a kinsman, and spoke:

"I am not dead but taken away into the fairy realm. When my wife bears the child she is carrying, and takes him to the Kirk to be christened, know that I will appear that day. Command my cousin, Graham of Duchray, to cast a dagger over my head and this alone will release me and allow me to return to the world of men. Do not fail to do as I say."

The message was conveyed to Graham of Duchray, and, true to what the apparition had said, on the day of the christening, Robert Kirk could be seen, standing in the Kirk behind his wife and newborn son.

Duchray raised the dagger, drew back his arm to throw it, but at the last, his nerves failed him and trembling, he hesitated.

"Throw it, man, throw it. Quickly!" urged Robert. Still Duchray hesitated, and in the silence of the Kirk, a cry of anguish came from the apparition, and then it vanished.

And so, Robert Kirk was taken once more by the hidden folk deep into Doon Hill.

"Maybe where he belongs," muttered Morag.

Some of you may doubt this strange story, but when Robert's wife, Isobel, died three years later, and her body laid beside that of her late husband, it was found that Robert's coffin was empty.

It is the belief of some people to this day that Robert Kirk remains in the Secret Commonwealth with the hidden folk, waiting, waiting for someone to free him so that he can return at last to his parish at Aberfoyle.

BOB MITCHELL

Bob Mitchell was born and brought up on a small croft in rural Aberdeenshire. He trained as a psychiatric nurse in the late 1960s and is long since retired from his post as senior lecturer (mental health) at Edinburgh's Napier University.

Currently the Chair of Burgh Blatherers, Bob is a busy storyteller and occasional writer of poetry and prose "Chiefly in the Scottish Dialect." He is a regular participant in the annual Buchan Heritage Festival which is based in his native North-East and promotes all aspects of its culture.

He is active in Burns circles and in this, their centenary year, he is President of the prestigious Poosie Nansie Burns Club based in Newcraighall in the outskirts of Edinburgh.

Bob lives in Haddington, East Lothian and has been married to Anne for forty-nine years. They have three grown up children, five grandchildren and a dog.

WHERE THERE'S A WILL

Bob Mitchell

I am told that versions of this tale were told some three thousand years ago in ancient Arabia but I have brought it bang up to date and set in surroundings very familiar to me, a small Aberdeenshire croft nestling at the back o' Bennachie, a well-known landmark in the North East of Scotland.

And there it was that three brothers lived, eking out a living in the same inhospitable terrain where they had lived their entire life and where their parents had worked their fingers to the bone many years before that.

The oldest brother, fast approaching thirty, had been christened Alexander but had always been known as Ecky. The second brother was called John but everywhere, he was called Jakey and the youngest brother was called Sebastian. Unfortunately, Sebastian had a chronic eye condition which meant that he had worn glasses since early childhood and so invariably, he was known as Specky!

Now neither, Ecky, Jakey nor Specky were married but they had been their own masters for some ten or twelve years by the time my tale begins and even though it was almost impossible to make a smallholding of that size economically viable all three were perfectly happy with their lot and would not have swapped places with anyone, not even a millionaire!

And then disaster struck! Since it turned out that the brothers had never owned their croft, but like their parents before them, they had rented it from some mysterious landlord that none of them had ever clapped eyes on.

Well did he not go and die. Without as much as a 'by your leave'. And that's when they heard about the Will!

Now clearly the landlord was something of an eccentric and may even have thought it all a great big joke, but it was no joke for Ecky, Jakey or Specky. Because this is what it said.

The landlord was going to set the brothers a riddle and if they could work out the answer, the croft and any money he may have set aside would be theirs, no questions asked. But if the brothers could not come up with the solution, everything would go to the 'Society for Wayward Homing Pigeons' away down in Edinburgh's new town. This was a charity very close to the landlord's heart since he had lost several of his own pigeons as a boy and had never quite got it over it.

And this was the puzzle. Amongst other things, the landlord had seventeen sheep that he promised to leave to the brothers, but they were not all to get the same amount. Ecky was to get half of them, Jakey had to get a third of them and Specky was to get a ninth of them or else the pigeons would get everything the landlord owned and the brothers would be homeless.

Oh, and the sheep could not be harmed in any way during the exercise and they could not simply be sold off and the money shared out.

Well, the problem was far too much for the brothers to get their heads round and so Ecky, Jakey and Specky took themselves off to see the Dominie, the Headmaster of the local school but he was worse than useless. He just blethered on about the evils of the computer age and said if they had all been living fifty years ago, he would simply have walloped them with his tawse since that had never done anyone any harm (in his opinion). And if they had any more stupid questions they should go and ask the Minister since he had an awful lot more time for such nonsense, with him only working one day in the week. But the minister turned out to be as useless as the Dominie and when he fell back on his usual explanation of "things moving in mysterious ways" Ecky, Jakey and Specky began to feel that they were indeed doomed.

Unless, hang on, there was one other educated person about the place and he was supposed to be exceptionally clever. He had arrived all the way from the University of Edinburgh with a bunch of young student lasses and for the last two or three months they had been out on the braes o' Bennachie every morning, counting and then photographing all the heaps of rabbit "poo" that had appeared during the night before entering it all into their specially programmed tablets. Apparently, it was called research and one of the students had been telling everyone in the pub the other night that it would prove ground-breaking. But it turned out he couldn't help the brothers with their puzzle either. He had "more important things to do," he said before getting straight back to his photographing and counting. Well, I suppose everyone is entitled to their opinion!

And that looked as if it was that as far as the brothers and the roof over their heads were concerned when who should appear but Donald, a simple youth who lived with his grandmother in a cottage on a neighbouring farm, with his pet lamb (now well and truly a ewe) trailing on behind him like the collie dog it maybe thought it was.

Donald was the very last person that the brothers needed right now.

"Away you go and don't annoy us," said the usually placid Ecky, "we've got far too much on our plates to bother about the likes of you."

But Donald was well used to being given a hard time and didn't seem to take any notice.

"A wee birdie tells me you might be needing a bit hand," he said, amicably. "Well just muck oot your lugs and listen tae me."

And it turned out that he had heard all about the brothers' predicament and what's more, he thought he had worked out an answer.

"What we'll hae to do," said Donald, "Is gie you a shot o' my wee ewie here."

Well, Ecky, Jakey and Specky wouldn't hear of it. They knew the sheep had been given to Donald two or three years ago when it was just a small orphan lamb and it had been his only friend ever since. They couldn't possibly take it off him, - no way. Besides, they didn't know where it had been!

But Donald's next question made them change their minds.

"Whaur are you thinking o' bidin' when the lawyers throw you oot?' he asked.

The brothers relented.

"Get on with it," they said.

"Fair enough," said Donald. "The landlord had seventeen sheep, and when I gie him my one, that makes eighteen."

"Well, he can count that much," said the brothers with some surprise.

"Noo, Ecky," he continued, "You've got tae get half o' them. What's half o' eighteen? Dinnae bother, I'll tell you, it's nine. You take your nine."

Ecky was delighted to get his share sorted out.

"Noo, Jakey, you were supposed to get a third o' them, and we a' ken a third o' eighteen is six. There's yours, Jakey, and that leaves three." The brothers were beginning to take notice.

"Noo, that leaves three and you had to get a ninth of them and a ninth o' eighteen is two. Go on Specky, help yourself.

And that just leaves my ain wee ewie, and none of you wanted her anyway, so I'll just hang on to her."

Donald had saved the day - the riddle was solved!

And so Ecky, Jakey and Specky inherited the smallholding after all and as it turned out the landlord had also amassed considerable savings and that was theirs as well. And the first thing they did with their new-found wealth was to give Donald a job sorting out their accounts and tax affairs because that was something at which they had always been hopeless. It was Donald's first job and he was so proud of himself.

The Dominie and the Minister kept their heads well down for a while, each convinced that given a bit more time they would have worked out the answer: before the other one.

And what about the man from the University? Well, he headed back down the road to Edinburgh and funnily enough, his research did turn out to be ground-breaking. The academic boffins were all delighted with it, and he ended up writing a scientific paper and getting a few more letters after his name. Quite delighted with himself, he was.

And that just left the rabbits. And as far as I know they're still leaping around the back o' Bennachie dropping their deposits or should that be depositing their droppings exactly where and when they please. Just as they've always done!

DORIS HART

A retired English professor, living in New York, she loves writing plays, stories and has been visiting Scotland for more than twenty-five years where she is a part-time in person member of the Blatherers. Covid did allow her to become a full-time Zoom member however, which is some small compensation.

MONKEY BUSINESS

Doris Hart

COVID did it! I was stuck in New York and couldn't return to Edinburgh where I'd been coming for twenty-five years. I had to escape. How? I sat down and wrote story after story, many of them about animals. Why animals? I'm fascinated by the way animals behave.

Look at them. Staring at me like I'm some Hindu god. Wish their mamas wouldn't send them to me. They believe I have some magic skills. But honestly anyone could learn to do this. No one taught me. I just figured it out.

Thank goodness there's only five of them this time. But that little one on the right. Can't be more than two. Not ready for this. But his big brother insists the little one's a fast learner. Oh well.

"Okay, youngsters. The best way to do this is get right into the action. That's my motto: 'Learn by doing'. So, when the next tall ones come, leap down from the temple and grab whatever you can; anything they hold or wear. Any questions?"

"Won't they be angry?"

"Of course they'll be angry. That's the point. That's when the fun begins. If they want those things back, they have to give us food. You'll see how this works."

So we were perched on the roof of this old temple, when, finally, we heard crunching sounds of an object coming toward us. The one who calls himself the Temple Guide said it was a bus.

"Here come the visitors," he calls and sure enough about ten tall ones climb out of the bus.

He calls to them and says:

"You must be careful. Put all your things inside a zipped bag and tie the bag tightly around your waist."

"Why do we have to do that?"

"You see those macacques atop the roof? They'll grab anything they can get their paws on."

"Oh they're so cute," one tall one cries out.

"They may be cute, but they're clever thieves."

A few of them follow the guide's advice, but most don't and quickly take out cameras and phones. I turn to my group.

"When they get close, I'll raise my right paw. That's the signal to grab what you can."

In a matter of seconds, we snatched what we could from the alarmed visitors.

I grunted with pleasure as they cried out: "They stole my …"

My little group and I returned to the roof to look over our booty. A few held up a phone, another a pair of sunglasses, and the little one held up a cap. I explained the phones were the best - lots of good food. Not so much for the sunglasses and the hat almost nothing. So now the Temple guide was explaining to the tall ones that they could rescue their things by offering us food.

"What kind of food?"

"They eat anything. They're omnivorous. Got any fruit or sweets or sandwiches?"

Several of them scurried back to the bus and retrieved bags of food. One of them held up a banana and we ignored that. The guide told them they'd have to bargain with us and offer much more for each item. The bargaining went on at least ten minutes until we agreed to exchange all the items.

"Not bad," I told my group. "Well done for a first time," and I handed out five bags of nuts, 12 bananas, and I kept two peanut butter sandwiches for myself.

Not long after, we saw another bus rolling up.

"Okay youngsters, we'll do one more and call it a day."

We sat at attention as the Temple Guide called out his warnings as the visitors approached. I gave the signal and we swooped down. There was a lot of confusion and screaming as we grabbed objects and we leaped back onto the Temple roof. But when we looked down, one of the tall visitors had grabbed the little one, who was shrieking and trying to pull free.

"Hey, you monkeys, give us back our things. Or we'll eat this little one."

I had to restrain big brother from leaping down.

The Temple Guide approached us below. "Hand over the goods," he commanded.

We hesitated and I pointed to the little one still struggling to escape.

"I'll make sure you get him back. Give me what you stole."

We had no choice and handed the things down to the guide. But when the guide returned the stolen objects, the tall man refused to release the little one.

"I hear these monkeys are very tasty."

The guide became angry, and they shouted, and it looked like they might start punching each other. Half the group cried out: "Give him the monkey." The other half shouted, "Keep the monkey."

Finally, the guide ran to the front of the bus and yelled at the driver,

"You will not move this bus until the baby macaque is freed. Even if we stay here all night. That's an order!"

And that made the tall one release the little one who fled back to us and leaped into his brother's arms. Well, I had enough. I sent that whole group back to their mamas.

From now on I'll run a one-monkey business.

RONA BARBOUR

Scottish, and from a long line of Storytellers, Rona was born in Glasgow one of eight children to registered blind parents and as a result she quickly learned the value and importance of communicating with others through story from an early age. Rona is a strong advocate for resurrecting storytelling within families and in schools. She writes several of her own works and also has a huge repertoire of stories including love stories, spine chilling ghost stories, traditional and fairy tales.

Rona has enjoyed a long career as a storyteller both in commerce and in education. Using storytelling as her medium she has worked in schools, colleges and universities all over the UK and abroad. A lifetime's study of the human psyche and human behaviour has armed her with the knowledge that stories can and do change lives. She is now based in Altrincham, England where all of her five children live nearby so she has access to her adored six grandchildren. She returns to her roots regularly to work and visit family in Scotland. As Director of the Board of The Society for Storytelling for 6 years, Rona travelled far and wide including The Middle East, Russia, Cyprus and Italy where she regularly hosts storytelling workshops.

THE GREEK WEAVERS

Rona Barbour

This is one of my very favourite stories.

All villages in Greece are beautiful, although some a little more than others and Ari's village was one of those - except a strange element of this particular village was that although it was almost always bright, sunny and warm in that area, there was always a huge puddle on the road up to the village which nobody could explain. No matter how many times they cleared it away, even dug down deep to the dry area, it always came back even when there had been no rain for months. Geologists and all sorts of interesting people came to examine the area to see if they could find an answer, but they always left baffled, no nearer to finding out than the last people who came to "fix" it had been.

Actually, the puddle has nothing to do with the story I am going to tell you, but I just thought you should know about it, so there, I've told you.

The other main attraction in the village was a young girl, the aforementioned Ari, a seventeen-year-old who was of such remarkable beauty that people came to see if she really was as beautiful as was proclaimed. It is doubtful if they would have come if it was just her beauty that was said to be remarkable as there are a great many Greek beauties, but Ari also possessed a great gift. She was an amazing weaver, and it was said that the characters in her tapestries where so lifelike, they looked as if they could step right out of the scene.

However, there was another less positive distinguishing feature of Ari and that was that she was a most unpleasant young woman. Sullen, and disrespectful to her elders especially her own mother who she would often be heard arguing with.

Her mother was deeply concerned for Ari and warned her about her behaviour and suggested she should be more thankful for her good fortune, especially the gift she has been given by the Gods.

"I don't believe in all that nonsense," Ari would say, "If the Gods really exist why don't they show themselves?"

One day she overstepped the mark when saying as usual what a great weaver she was and how pretty she was and if the Gods really did exist, she bet that she would be prettier than any of them and a better weaver too....

Unfortunately for her, Athena, who was said to be the most beautiful of all the Gods and also a very talented weaver, overheard this. She was furious.

"Who is this upstart of a girl? She needs to be taught a lesson; I will pay her a visit."

And so it was that just a few days later, Athena, dressed as an old beggar woman, arrived on the road to Ari's village. Encountering the famous puddle, she just lifted herself off the ground, glided over it and carried on up the hill. When she reached the home of Ari and her mother, she knocked loudly.

Ari ran to answer it and when she opened the door, she looked the old lady up and down.

"Who are you? What do you want?"

"Well, my dear," said Athena, "I've come to see you and look at your tapestries, I believe you are supposed to be quite a good weaver may I have a look?"

Ari hesitated.

"Well, if you are not going to buy one, why should I let you see them?"

Ari's mother appeared at the door just then and berated her daughter for her rudeness and invited the "Old Lady" in.

"I am sorry," she said to Athena. "My daughter has much to learn about how to treat people especially her Elders."

"Well now that she is here," said Ari, "I bet she will want to have one of my tapestries, but I doubt she can afford one so show her out mother." Athena was furious but kept her cool.

"Actually, I can see that you are a wonderful weaver my dear, but I think I am better."

"What did you say, are you mad?" Ari cried. "You are just a stupid, ugly old woman."

"No, my dear I'm not mad, I challenge you to show who is best. Or are you afraid of the competition?"

"Absolutely not," said Ari. "Name your challenge," she scoffed.

"Very well," said Athena. "We shall both weave a tapestry depicting the Geek Gods and whoever makes the best job of that shall be the winner."

"And who should be the Judge?" Said Ari.

"I think your mother would be the perfect judge, don't you?"

Ari's mother went to say something, but Ari stopped her in her tracks.

"Yes, mother that is a great idea, you can do something useful for a change."

Athena was furious but kept herself in check, "Not yet," she said to herself.

"I will be back in three days, and we will decide then who is the best weaver," She said to Ari.

"Three days, that's too long," said Ari. "Let's make it two".

"Very well, two it is," agreed Athena and excused herself, curtsied to Ari's mother, and left.

After she had gone, Ari's mother told her off for the way she had treated the "old woman".

"You have no respect for anyone or anything Ari, not even the Gods, and that worries me Ari."

"There you go again," said Ari. "I told you I don't believe the Gods are real but even if they were, I don't believe that they are any better than you or me or are any more beautiful than me and certainly not a better weaver amongst them than I am."

Unfortunately for Ari, Athena of course was watching and listening to her and if she was angry before, there was smoke coming out of her ears now and her eyes, even her mouth too, she looked like she might explode.

Two days later she was back at Ari's home, was warmly greeted by Ari's mother and shown into the living room of the small villa. She could see that Ari's mother was upset and nervous and when she spoke it was to plead to Athena to understand that her daughter was young and foolish and didn't know any better.

"Please don't be angry with my silly daughter dear lady for she is no more than a foolish child."

Athena quickly saw why the old Ari's mother was so upset.

Ari had woven the most incredible tapestry depicting all the Greek Gods and Goddesses including herself. However, she had made caricatures of them which were quite startling: King Zeus had been drawn with a huge wart on his nose and was cross-eyed; Apollo had donkey's ears; Poseidon had a face like a fish; Dionysus looked drunk. Aphrodite looked hideously ugly; Pan looked like a gnome and she herself had been given a full-blown moustache. It was so clever and so funny that at the same time Athena really did want to laugh but she was too incensed at the temerity of this idiot of a girl, having the audacity to portray her family like this.

In a rage she stamped her foot, and the noise she made was so loud that Ari and her mother let out a cry and suddenly, standing before them, was the Goddess Athena.

Ari fell to her feet and immediately started to beg for mercy.

"I am so sorry your greatness," she cried, not knowing how to address Athena.

"Oh no my dear, you don't know what sorry is, but you are about to find out. You were born with two wonderful gifts, your beauty which is quite magnificent and your talent for weaving which I must agree with you, is better than mine. However, I am going to punish you for this insult to my family and for your total lack of respect for everyone, especially your dear mother, so, I am going to take one of those gifts from you."

There was no need now, for Ari's mother to judge.

"Oh please, take my weaving," cried Ari. "Otherwise I cannot go to Athens and find a rich husband, no one will want me if I am ugly."

"You are so right about that my dear, but I am going to let you keep your weaving because you are going to need that, more than ever now. I shall take your beauty."

With that, Athena put her hand on Ari's head and started to press down. As she did so, Ari got smaller and smaller until she was on the floor, just the size of a small coin and with a few words from Athena, eight great long hairy legs sprouted from that little fat body and two huge red eyes sprouted from the side of her head.

"You will live in dark corners, where you will weave yourself a home and everyone will hate and despise you, I will give you a mate who will also despise you, but you will have many young and each of them will have many young too until you, and your kind will be spread the world over."

Ari's mother was sobbing in the corner until Athena went towards her, put her hands on her shoulders and said a few words which made Ari's mother disappear. She would wake up the next day in a whole different world, with a different family and absolutely no recollection of ever having been married and widowed before and no recollection whatsoever of her horrible daughter Ari.

Athena turned her attention again to Ari.

"I believe your full name is Arachne, a pretty name for such an ugly creature but I shall let you keep that too."

And so it was, that the first spider on earth was made and one young weaver was taught a very hard lesson.

Athena left the village the same way as she had arrived, and, as she left, she took the offending puddle with her, I don't know why but maybe it offended her too, or maybe… it was just because she could.

It must be said that Athena not only punished Ari for her wrongdoings, she also, probably unwittingly one would hope, punished those amongst us who have had to live with a fear of spiders all of our lives. But then Athena was known to sometimes do that sort of thing just because she was a Goddess, and just because she could.

FINDLAY TAYLOR

Findlay was born, and lived until he was twelve, in Cambuskenneth, a village on the outskirts of Stirling. His family moved to Edinburgh where Findlay still carried on his enjoyment of outdoor life and his love of animals. He worked for a large telecoms company and his speciality was external works. Married with children and grandchildren he enjoys walking, camping and canoeing with them. Now retired he still enjoys the outdoor life and has taken up dog walking professionally as well as helping out on a livery.

One day during the festival in Edinburgh he decided to do something different. He visited the Scottish Storytelling Centre. There, to his surprise, he found he loved listening and watching storytellers. He decided wanted to learn the skill. This led him to become a storyteller himself and compile his own stories, always with animals in them.

LOVE

Findlay Taylor

This is one of my own tales. It is based on my love for outdoors particularly walking the Pentland hills with their tremendous views and of course, my love for animals. I now live in a village called Juniper Green, a half hour walk from Bonaly, on the very edge of Edinburgh and wake up every morning looking out to the Pentland hills – I walk these paths in all weathers and like to imagine the lives of those who have gone before…

"Love is the most powerful and still most unknown energy in the world." – Pierre Teilhard de Chardin

Jock was born in the 1700s. He grew up to become a shepherd as was his father and his father's father. He lived in a hamlet called Bonaly, which is situated on the north side of the Pentland hills, overlooking the capital of Scotland, Edinburgh. At that time the hamlet consisted of the Laird's house and three cottages for the weaver, the farrier and the shepherd.

Jock had been born and brought up in Bonaly and at the time of the story, there were his wife Ella, his son John and himself in the cottage and of course, his two collie sheepdogs.

Jock loved his family and his sheep almost equally. He loved being a shepherd, caring for his sheep and roaming the Pentland hills. Jock would take his young son up to the hills to show him how to look after the sheep and learn their habits, where they like to graze depending on the weather and season. Jock would also explain the view from the Pentlands. Looking north, Edinburgh with its castle and volcanic rock called Arthur's Seat. Beyond Edinburgh, the river Forth weaving its way into the North Sea and Europe. On the other side of the river, The Kingdom of Fife and the Highlands. Jock was happy in his own parish, with all this spread out before him.

As John got older, he and his father would drove the sheep 7 miles to the market in Edinburgh. John was surprised at all the noise, the smells, the different people there, he was fascinated by it all. Jock, on the other hand, was always a bit sad and tearful having to sell his sheep and happy to return to his hills.

One day, when Jock and John were walking the Pentlands, the lad told his father he had decided to leave home to join the army and see the world. Ella was not pleased about the news and tried to persuade her son not to go, but Jock was not surprised. He felt the boy was restless and not ready to settle down to a shepherd's life. The following day John said his goodbyes and walked away down the road and up to Edinburgh castle to sign up with the Edinburgh Volunteers.

As the years passed by, brother soldiers would come to tell Jock and Ella how John was doing and where he was, travelling the Americas and Europe in far-flung wars, but he himself stayed away.

One year in March, just at the time when lambs are born, a terrific storm came. Jock had never seen such snow at this time of year and was very fretful about his sheep and lambs. He spent the day on the hills, herding his sheep to the safety of the pen adjacent to his cottage. Finally, early in the evening, he settled down to his tea when he realised he had forgotten to check Maiden's Cleugh, a favourite sheltering place for his sheep. To his wife's horror the shepherd decided he was going back out with his sheepdog to check for any missing sheep. She tried to persuade him not to go. It was still snowing, and the snow was drifting deep with the wind, but to no avail. He was going. Ella knew she would stay up for his return and ensure the fire was still burning, with hot broth ready for him on.

The following morning the cottage door opened. Ella woke up from her chair where she had waited the night through. Her first thought was Jock was back at last but, to her surprise, it was not Jock but her son, John. Oh, how delighted she was to see him. She had missed him so much. He had precious days home on leave but due to the weather he had stayed the night in Edinburgh. Ella told him about Jock and John immediately said he would go and look for him.

John set off with the old collie Bess, who he himself had trained as a boy in years before with his father. It was a beautiful sunny morning, clear blue skies after the stormy night. As he climbed up from Bonaly to Harbour Hill he stopped and looked North. He felt home at last. The sight of Edinburgh in the distance and seeing the tall ships in Newhaven harbour. He even reckoned he could make out the ship on which he had returned to Edinburgh. Looking west he could see the Ochil hills and up to the Trossachs.

On he went into Maiden's Cleugh - well named as this was where his Mum and Dad had pursued their courting. He then headed south towards Glen Corse and the church his parents had gotten married in. All the time he and Bess were looking for signs of his father. They checked the church in case his dad was sheltering there with no luck.

Onto Knightfield Rigg, a derelict cottage where his great-great-grandfather had lived, now in ruins, roofless, just a pile of stones. Bess suddenly started barking and making for the old cottage. Against the old walls was a large drift piled up where Bess barked and barked and scratched at the snow. John cleared the ground and found his father's dog, his father and then the ewe all lying, huddled and lifeless together.

John fell to the ground and cried. While in the wars he had killed, and soldiers had tried to kill him. He had seen the atrocities of war both on and off the battlefield. He had seen what soldiers would do to others with no care or remorse. He saw what they did to men, women and children who were completely innocent. The damage that was done to buildings and crops, all in the name of war. The number of times he had stepped in to try and stop the cruelty to others that sickened him, but in time he got hardened to the ways of a soldier's life.

Even so, he had promised himself he would never tell his parents of what had happened abroad.

What he saw before him was what the world should be about - love and caring for others.

The love of collie dog for his master. Always totally loyal to his master giving his life for him. John remembered when he fell into a river his dad's collie was straight in to help him to get out heedless of danger. A death from love instead of another senseless death from war.

And the love of his father for his sheep. All these years his dad had looked after the sheep whether they were ill or the lambs needed mothering - he was there. He had died as he had lived and though John was sad and shocked, he knew his father had made his own choice.

John heard a sound like movement from under the ewe. He thought he was hearing things, but the noise got louder and eventually a very muffled Ba, Ba, Ba. It was a newly born lamb being protected by its mother even in death. It was a beautiful new life come through the storm and innocent of what had happened to its mother.

John picked it up and put it inside his coat. He headed for home. The lamb needed milk, heat and, of course, love.

John climbed through Phantom's Cleugh valley and onto the ridge above Bonaly. Standing on the ridge he looked down on Bonaly and the surrounding hills and he knew he was done with the army. He would not be signing on again and would never again stray far from these hills where such love was the way of death and life.

LYNSEY WRIGHT

I come from a long line of fibbers, exaggerators and fantastical thinkers. I was born and grew up in the North East of Scotland. My father and uncle were great storytellers. It was not traditional stories they told but personal stories of family and friends. We never tired of hearing them, no matter how many times they were told. When I was nineteen, I came to Edinburgh to study and became a primary school teacher. I used stories a lot in my work and built up a library of traditional stories. We would have storytelling events in school and encourage children to share their own stories. When I retired, I decided I wanted to learn more of the art of storytelling and joined storytelling groups and completed the apprentice scheme at the Storytelling Centre, keeping storytelling an important part of my life.

WET! WET! WET!

Lynsey Wright

This story is just a bit of fun and I have no idea where I got the idea from. I told it so many times when I was teaching and it became part of my repertoire.

Donald was seated on top of Blackford Hill gazing down at the beautiful view and the people below. They were laughing and joking and he felt his spirits sink. He was a giant and wherever he went people felt afraid of him and kept their distance.

It was a very lonely life being a giant.

He had fallen in love with a young woman called Eilidh who lived below, and she had fallen in love with him, but it was a love that was going nowhere. He towered over her and when he spoke to her, he had to bend down and pick her up and whisper in her ear which was very tickly and made her laugh. If she needed to speak to him, he had to lift her up and of course when she shouted in his ear it also meant that he burst out laughing.

This was no way to conduct a romance and with a heavy heart he decided he had to end the relationship with Eilidh. He had heard that up in the north-west of Scotland there lived a giant, a lady who was as tall as he was, and he was going to head up there to see if she could be his next love. He left the next day and made good progress and by lunchtime he was halfway there beside a deep, fast flowing river.

He had to cross the river, and this was causing him some worries.

When he was young he had never been good at listening to his mother. He vaguely remembered a conversation she had had

52

with him, and it had been very important and had something to do with water, but he could recall nothing about their talk.

As he hesitated, he realised that halfway across the river was a sandbank with a huge whale stuck there in some distress. Now, should he head into the river and release the whale? Of course he should! He stepped into the water, waded towards the whale and pushed it off its prison into much deeper water. The whale gave a joyful splash and asked Donald where he was going because he could take him there.

This was such an unusual day that Donald did not think it strange that a whale could speak. He told the whale his story and where he was heading and climbed on. At first the whale struggled with Donald's weight but soon they began moving through the water quite quickly. It was not long before they had reached their destination.

Donald climbed off the whale's back and he asked the whale if he could wait around in case things did not work out.

The whale said he would wait at an island which was about 20 km away.

Donald watched as the whale sped away and turned around when he heard a noisy racket coming from the hill opposite. Looking up he saw the biggest woman he had ever seen.

She was wearing huge workman's boots, a very short skirt which showed off her hairy knees nicely, a short cardigan full of holes and her hair was pulled on top of her head in a tight bun.

When she came nearer Donald, he realised that she towered over him.

"What are you doing here?" she thundered. Donald decided to be perfectly honest and replied, "I am looking for love and I had heard you were a giant like me." Donald felt quite ridiculous saying this as it was obvious that she towered over him.

She let out a laugh, bent down, picked Donald up by his hair, spun him round her head and sent him flying over the sea where he landed comfortably on the whale's back. There was nothing he could do but head back home.

When he got to the village where Eilidh lived he got the whale to stop and climbed off its back which proved quite difficult to do. What on earth was wrong with him? He waved goodbye and stood on the shore looking around.

He saw a figure running towards him and realised it was Eilidh, but now something had changed. She was only slightly smaller than him. She flung her arms around him and kissed him on the lips.

Eventually they stopped hugging, kissing and laughing and tried to fathom out what had happened.

Donald kept remembering about his mother's warnings about not going near water – the conversation he had never listened to.

Had somebody put a spell on him? Was there something in his genetics? But whatever had happened, he had shrunk!! Eilidh stepped back and regarded him with a serious look on her face.

"You must promise me you will never go back in the water again because I do not want my husband to end up the size of a thumb!"

And he never did go near water again.

JACKIE CAROTHERS

Jackie was born in India, grew up in England and worked in Nigeria, Germany, and London before moving to Edinburgh to work as a social worker in 1972. In Edinburgh she discovered storytelling through the Scottish Storytelling Centre and told her first story at the Good Crack Club, in Edinburgh's Waverley Bar. She is a founder member of the Burgh Blatherers Storytelling Group and of course she enjoys collecting and telling traditional tales from Scotland and around the world.

THE RUBY

Jackie Carothers

*The theme of this simple but powerful parable from the Hindu tradition
will probably be familiar to many of the four thousand Hindu people who
now live in Edinburgh, many of whom settled here in the second half of
the twentieth century.*

*After years of using hired premises and working hard to renovate a
suitable building, finally, in April 2015, members of the Hindu
community were able to celebrate the inauguration of the Edinburgh
Hindu Mandir (temple) and Cultural Centre, the induction of a full-time
priest, and the unveiling of magnificent marble statues of the Hindu
deities in the Temple Hall.*

*The Centre not only provides the Hindu community with opportunities for
worship, cultural arts and social activities but welcomes members of other
communities too, contributing richly to Edinburgh's cultural diversity.*

The old man slept the night at the edge of the village, lying
on the bare ground. Next morning, he woke, as usual, just
before dawn as the first birds began to sing; a gentle breeze
brushed his cheek, bringing with it the musky smell of moist
soil that heralds the Monsoon rains.

Fully awake now, he sat cross-legged, facing East as dawn
spread its light across the sky. Then he began his morning
meditation just as he had always done since he first became a
sadhu, a holy man, long ago.

Suddenly he heard hurried footsteps behind him and then a
voice

"Master, Master."

He turned ... and there stood a young villager, his chest
heaving up and down with excitement, his eyes eager and
intense.

The sadhu looked at the young man for a long moment.

"What is it you want from me, my son?"

"Master, last night I had a dream, and in that dream I came to the edge of the village, just here…. and I saw a holy man…. just like you. And in my dream the holy man gave me a precious jewel…"

"Aah" said the sadhu. He reached into his pouch and took out a ruby as big as a child's fist. "Maybe you mean this," (he opened his hand) "I found it somewhere, sometime, but I have no use for it. You may have it," and he gave the ruby to the young man.

The young man took the ruby in his two hands, one on top of the other, as the custom is when receiving a gift. He could not believe his good fortune: never before had he held more than two copper coins in these hands. Now he held the precious stone up to the sun, his face awash in its crimson light. Then, bowing low, he thanked the old man and walked slowly back to the village, cradling the ruby in his hands, his arms stretched out in front of him. He couldn't take his eyes off the jewel.

All day he sat on his small mat, just inside the door of his simple hut, gazing at his precious treasure. He would hold it up to the light, and then he'd turn it over in his hands, this way and that, stroking it slowly, reverently, feeling its smoothness, learning its shape … delighting in its beauty as the hours passed until darkness fell.

That night the young man couldn't sleep.

Early next morning he set out to catch up on his work in the fields, with the ruby safe in his pocket. He came to the place where he'd met the sadhu the day before and found the old man was still there, in the same place, meditating. He went up to the sadhu and they greeted each other. The young man took the ruby out of his pocket and gave it back to the sadhu.

"Thank you for this precious gift. But I know now that this is not what I want."

"Ah," replied the holy man "And what is it that you want?"

"I want what you know that makes it easy for you to give away such a precious jewel."

INTERVAL

Well! Well, well. What did you think of that? How do you feel? It's a real treat that you're here.

What an evening. And we are only half way through. Let's mix and mingle.

Stories! We all tell them. How was your day? What did you see on your way? What's that you say about your dog, your aunt, the contents of your pocket? Hey! Everyone is telling stories all around us.

Tales. They tell us who we are, who we might become. They show us our terror and hold our hope, carry us into the mysteries of this world and beyond. They are always behind us, with us, before us.

In fact, there are more starting up just now.

Come, let's go back in for more. Bring your drink with you.

Who's next?

Bob!

"On yonder hill,
There stands a doocot.
It's nae there noo,
Somebody's took it."

"Ladies and gentlemen, thank you for returning so promptly and welcome to the second half of tonight's entertainment. I hope you all managed to avail yourself of some of the Haggis Box's delights. Perhaps, most delightful of all, you availed yourself of a small tot of their whisky – our national drink.

My attitude to whisky has long been influenced by the advice given to me by an uncle on his deathbed. "Never," he advised, "drink whisky without first adding water. And never drink water without first adding whisky."

I loved that man and have always regretted that he was taken from us far too soon. Aged twenty-nine. Cirrhosis of the liver. And trouble with his waterworks.

But now, "On with the show!"

Jill McPherson has a tale which contains not a trace of whisky but which does involve a fair stretch of water.

Jill!"

JILL MCPHERSON

Jill McPherson spent half her childhood in Edinburgh and the other half on the Isle of Skye, where she still has family and visits regularly. She loves both deeply and finds them equally inspiring, especially stories with a Skye connection. She has a passion for telling tales for and about young women sharing them in her role as a Girl Guiding leader. She inherited a love of music from her paternal grandmother Chrissie and her development as a fiddle player remains a work in progress.

THE INVASION OF INCHCOLM

Jill McPherson

Storytellers are sometimes asked who told them stories as a child. My roots go back to my maternal grandmother who regularly had us in tears of laughter with her tales, all of which were said to be true, though she once admitted to adding bits 'to help the story along'.

My other influence was my paternal grandfather Mac McPherson, whose steady stream of Sunday post jokes and wee songs – the Cupar of Fife being a favourite – had us giggling and rolling our eyes. He married Chrissie. When I knew her as 'granny' she behaved like a quintessential Edinburgh lady, complete with twinset and pearls, and was very firm and correct with us. Like many ladies of her age, she had problems with her 'waterworks' and she repeatedly warned my sisters and I of how to avoid a similar fate. The cause, she told us, was long waits at cold, windy Edinburgh bus stops during the war while wearing French Knickers. Mac himself was a big personality, entrepreneurial and at times a bit of a handful as this story shows.

When World War II started, Edinburgh suffered its share of bombing raids. My Dad, Mac's son, remembers as a toddler seeing a German bomber flying along the Forth and being taken down to the Anderson Shelter his father had constructed in the garden.

As a builder, Mac was not conscripted but stayed in Edinburgh and did war work, including building some of the fortifications on Inchcolm Island in the Firth of Forth. Multiple gun emplacements and buildings were being put in place to defend the east coast in the event of an invasion. Being work for the military, it was tightly specified. Mac, a man who felt rules were for other folks who needed them as they couldn't think for themselves, was possibly not in his most natural element.

Every day he would sail out with Frank the Foreman, his team, and supplies to Inchcolm. What he didn't know (it was top secret at the time) was that the Forth fortifications were part of a successful ruse, codenamed Operation Fortitude, to trick Hitler into thinking an allied invasion of Europe (what became D Day) would be launched from sites including south east Scotland landing at destinations including south Norway.

Not surprisingly, security around the building job was tight. The Navy was on edge, regularly patrolling looking out for German vessels. All contractor boats had to display coloured lights as a security code. The combination changed each day, a simple but effective rule.

To add to the tension, there was huge nervousness around protecting the ruins of twelfth century Inchcolm Abbey. Mac was dead chuffed when he managed to adapt a tractor by setting the wheels inward so that its footprint was slim enough to pass through a narrow entrance in the ruins he needed to use to get his construction materials to the site.

It was a lot to juggle. And so it was that after another pressured day, he and his team set sail from Inchcolm to return home. Winter was coming in and it was already dark. The east wind was cutting through. He was looking forward to dinner and wondering what morsels Chrissie his wife had managed to get from the butchers with her ration coupons and a bit of eyelash-batting. Suddenly he heard a shout from Frank.

He looked round and there, coming towards them at speed, looming overhead in the darkness was the outline of what looked like a warship. Due to the blackout, there were few lights. As it approached, the wash from the bows set Mac's boat lurching from side to side. He looked up and could see the outline of a military gun barrel outlined against the sky. It was pointing at him.

Out of the darkness, from the direction of the warship, came a commanding voice with a German-sounding accent.

"Halt!"

Just what he needed, the bl**dy Germans. The boats were surging up and down in the bow wash, the gun still pointing at Mac's wee boat.

Deciding that he wouldn't go quietly, forefinger in the air to make his point, Mac yelled back a useful German insult he'd learned from a seaman in a bar in Leith.

"Der Weihnachtsmann kommt!"

He had no idea what it meant, but it really packed a punch and it seemed to do the trick.

There was a pause. The vessels still surged up and down. The east wind was getting between his ribs now.

From the warship, he heard crisp tones, in received pronunciation say:

"Captain, he seems to be German."

"Ay," yelled back Mac. "And if I'm German you must be Colonel Blimp!"

A few minutes later a Royal Navy launch, also armed, slowly approached his vessel and six seamen boarded. After demanding Mac's name and details, they pointed to the security lights.

"What is today's code?" One of the navy men was pointing a rifle at him.

Mac looked up at the lights and calmly read them off … red, yellow, unlit, blue.

"Are you sure?"

Mac pointed cheekily to his lights. As he turned, he could see Frank frantically waving a piece of paper at him. Mac grabbed it and read it out. It was another security code: unlit, yellow, unlit, blue.

The man pointing the rifle moved a step closer.

"Mr McPherson, unless you wish to finish the day as a prisoner of war, I need today's code."

Throughout his life, Mac always had a wee bit of paper and a wee pencil to hand for useful notes. Mac could see that in the wheelhouse, Frank was frantically rifling through a considerable pile of wee bits of paper.

Eventually, he emerged with one, the correct date was confirmed, and the code given: unlit, yellow, green, blue.

After the appropriate admonishment had been given, the navy launch and its crew left. Mac climbed up to switch on the right combination of lights, muttering about jobsworths, and Frank watched the naval gun pull away from their wee boat, and headed the bow for home.

It had all been a misunderstanding and Mac had not had to rely on his blood curling German insult to ensure his safe passage. Perhaps it is just as well, I am reliably assured that it translates into "Santa Claus is coming!"

Mac was a character, and we have a few tales about him. I can't remember if it was Mac or Granny Chrissie who told me this one. It's not known in the rest of the family, but of course that is not a problem. Where I didn't know something, I might have added a few bits to help the story along …

ANNE DIGNAN

Anne is still resident in Edinburgh where she was born and bred. She enjoys writing many of her own stories from historical research. She has been a member of Burgh Blatherers since 2019 and is currently developing her craft as storyteller on the Apprentice Storyteller scheme with the Scottish Storytelling Centre. Telling stories in the oral tradition has given her a deep sense of achievement since she became registered as visually impaired. A diagnosis of early onset Macular Degeneration led her to medical retirement from the world of education, but her new world has gained added dimensions inspired by her change in circumstances. Membership of Burgh Blatherers, telling stories both virtually and in person has greatly enriched her development as a storyteller, culminating in winning the Tall Tales Oscar at the Scottish Storytelling Centre in Scotland's Year of Stories 2022.

MEMORIAL TO LOST SOULS

Anne Dignan

As a citizen of Edinburgh born and bred I count myself lucky to say that we have some of the most incredible landscape and geology. We can boast our very own volcano as well, Arthur's seat (luckily for us, an extinct volcano!) A few years ago a piece was printed in the Scotsman about the curious discovery of miniature coffins on Arthurs' seat. After some research in the National Museum website this is my response to that curiosity.

It was in the year of 1836, Jaimie, his dog Snap, and his pals loved hunting rabbits on the hillside of Arthur's Seat.

They loved roaming free and wild hoping for a good catch that they could take round to the butcher's shop earning a penny for a brace of rabbits or to take home for their mother to cook. If only a few rabbits were caught, they each took turns as to whom would take a rabbit home for tea. This was most welcomed as their families lived hand to mouth in the squalor of the Auld Toun near the West Port.

Their fathers took any work that was going.

Not too far away some of the gentry still lived, cheek by jowl, although many had gone to live over the bridge in the fancy New Town which James Craig designed in 1766.

As the youngsters ran down the steep eastern slope of Arthur's Seat, Jaimie tripped and fell. As he was getting up, he noticed some triangular pointed slates. There were three of them, unusually shaped. Curiously, looking more closely, Jaimie pulled the slates apart to see what lay beyond.

Lo and behold there was a miniature cave!

Jaimie peered into the damp dank gloom and saw a tiny, long wooden box of about four inches with flat metal shapes adorning its lid. It reminded him of a miniature coffin.

"Come here lads! I've found a braw bit treasure and its no' rabbits doon a hole!"

Panting and scrambling Snap and the boys all gathered around this mysterious find.

"Hae a keek at thon," said Jaimie and he opened the box. Inside there was what looked like a wooden doll with no arms, two legs with flat feet and a detailed, carved face. The doll was swathed in a tunic and trousers sewn and glued tightly round the figure. It was swaddled in a bit of cloth.

Silence, then a flurry of frenzied excitement. Jaimie put his hand in once more and saw there was a layer of smaller slates like a floor. Gingerly he removed the slates and gasped. Before him lay eight similar wooden boxes packed tightly and with metal adorning their lids just like the first.

The other boys all wanted to grab the boxes, but Jaimie fought off their grasping hands and brought out each of the eight boxes quite carefully himself.

They prised open the lids amidst gasps of wonderment. They discovered that each box held a similar figure dressed in different patterned or plain fabrics, but some figures had their arms intact, lying stiffly at their sides. Each figure was also swaddled in a bit of cloth. There were similarities and yet each doll had its own distinctive character and design.

One of the other boys delved into the hole and carefully removed yet another layer of slates, and yet again amidst gasps and shrieks of delight, there lay another layer of these tiny wooden coffins.

There were eight coffins again in this layer and when the boys opened the tiny lids, they saw and smelt mouldering cloths swaddled around the detailed carved figures.

There were seventeen figures in total.

The boys stuffed the figures into their pocket and rabbit-chasing now long forgotten, ran away with the dog Snap at their heels.

The boys kept their treasure find a secret. People were jumpy and edgy about anything death related.

There remained deep unrest amongst the townsfolk who were battling to protect their dead from the resurrectionists or body snatchers who would rob graves by night to sell cadavers to one of the many anatomy schools within this great city of learning and enlightenment. Edinburgh was still dealing with the aftermath of the mass murderer William Burke who had been hanged in front of a crowd of thousands just a few years earlier in 1828. His accomplice William Hare had turned Kings evidence and was thus spared the gallows. Burke had been found guilty of the murders of seventeen people.

The God-fearing Christian folk strongly believed that if a corpse was interfered with in any way and not allowed to rest in the grave, then on the final Judgement Day the soul of that corpse would not rise up and be forgiven by the Lord. Such souls would not be allowed to pass into the Kingdom of Heaven and enjoy everlasting life. Many wealthy families had metal bars put over the graves, or a metal carapace into which a coffin would be placed to deter the grave robbers.

Now Jaimie's father drank in a local tavern in the West Port. This was in the very same street as the actual lodging house that William Hare had owned and where the first victim was murdered in 1827. The body of the deceased tenant was sold by Burke and Hare to the anatomists allegedly to recover a debt that the dead lodger owed William Hare.

Jaimie's father, Jock, often shared a dram with the local shoemaker, Tam Souter.

When the topic arose about the Burke and Hare murders it was acknowledged that they had not got involved in grave robbery to supply corpses to the medical schools, but that they had simply murdered victims in order to supply the anatomy tables directly. It gave them a lucrative income of around £10 a cadaver. As the grisly duo became greedier they became more careless. Some of the people they murdered were recognisably unique characters amongst the homeless and itinerant communities.

Tam Souter, a devout Christian and regular church attendee, often expressed deep vexation, anger, and anguish when talking about all the lost souls who met a brutal end and were condemned to death at the hand of Burke and Hare – Satan's apocalyptic servants.

Gradually Souter seemed to become obsessed with the murders and would either be very withdrawn and melancholic or be ranting and raving like a man possessed,

"Its no richt that thon innocent folks should be brutally feenished off and then be denied gaein tae the Lords Hoose in Heaven." This double injustice seeming to weigh heavily on his mind.

We'll leave the men to enjoy their ale and consider this most plausible of all the theories about the origin of the coffins.

Did Tam Souter attempt to give the seventeen murdered souls a sacred burial on the ancient sacred Arthur's Seat site, so they could enter the gates of Heaven on Judgement Day?

Was his Christian conscience assuaged?

Were the tiny coffins buried there to keep them safe from harm's way?

Many years later, long after Tam Souter and Jock were laid to rest, some of the coffins were offered to the Museum of Antiquities in 1901 from various private collections. Only eight were donated to the museum. The rest may have been accidentally destroyed by Jaimie and his pals, or perhaps they are still in private hands?

Around the time of the Millennium, Dr Allan Simpson at the National Museum of Scotland reviewed the evidence that the coffins had so far yielded and attempted to discover more about them.

All the coffins were carved from the same piece of wood, the tool used to gouge out the interior was very like the specialist knife a shoemaker would use, with a curved end. The little talismans on the coffin lids were akin to metal parts used in making shoe buckles. The threads stitching the clothing can be matched to three ply thread types first manufactured in Paisley around the 1830s and also the tiny pins attaching the lids to the coffins were handmade like shoemakers of the period would have used.

Perhaps the earlier theories of witchcraft, effigies of drowned sailors being buried in family graves and the customs in Saxony of burying effigies might be discounted.

The compelling conclusion for me is that the coffins were all constructed at the same time and lain to rest not longer than six years before they were discovered by the small boys. Regardless, the coffins have been on display almost constantly since their donation and are silent witnesses to a mysterious past.

ANNE PITCHER

Anne was born in Ayr, went to university three times in Glasgow, has lived in Switzerland, New Zealand and London. She has had many careers- newspaper journalist, community artist, public relations officer for a disabled charity, nursery manager, registered childminder, nursery teacher and is now a Traditional Arts and Culture Scotland Directory storyteller and Storytelling Forum member. Anne is married with two grown, married sons and two adored grandchildren. A world traveller, Anne enjoys different cultures, languages, learning and telling tales. Often, some of her collection of over six hundred puppets, unusual props and sound makers, accompany her tales. During Covid Anne discovered a talent for illustrative drawing and now often incorporates art into her storytelling. A life saver during Covid was joining online the delightful, distinctive, talented, Burgh Blatherers whose members have taken her into their midst even though her 'home' storytelling club is Glasgow Better Crack Club.

OLD MISERY GUTS AND DEATH

Anne Pitcher

I can't remember from whom I heard this story - it may have been Andy Hunter, a well-known Edinburgh teller, but to be honest I've heard it from so many sources in various forms that I think it's a traditional tale.

A long time ago there was once an old woman who lived on the outskirts of Blackford Hill. She was by herself in a big old house, and it had a large apple tree in her front garden which produced the most wonderfully delicious, round, red, rosy apples every year. All around her garden was a high wall to stop people scrumping these tasty apples, but it did not stop them trying. One big branch hung over the garden wall beside the path which went into the village and the ripe red fruits would dangle down invitingly to all who passed.

Wee boys in short trousers with skint knees, would give the smallest, lightest lad a punt up, to the nearest branch. He would stretch his hands up high and then stuff as many apples as he could into his pockets and his jumper. When 'Old Misery Guts', as they called her locally, saw what the wee laddies were up to, she shouted, shaking her fist in the air,

"Stop scrumping my apples ye wee toerags! I'll tell yer mammies!!" They would jump down, making faces, poking out their tongues and then run away, munching their prizes, shouting,

"Ha! Ha! Ha! Old Misery Guts!"

Then Auld Hamish would come hirpling along the path, on his daily walk, leaning on his wooden walking stick and would not be able to resist temptation. His mouth would water at the thought of one juicy bite of the apples. He remembered when

78

he was a young lad scrumping apples with delight. Hamish looked this way and that to check no-one could see him, balanced on his good leg and stretched his walking stick up, knocking an apple or two off the tree till Old Misery Guts came out and spotted him.

"Ye auld tyke, get away frae my tree," she shouted, "or I'll come and break yer stick ower yer heid!" Hamish would hirple off laughing heartily with an amazing spurt of speed.

One day a wee plump, old woman with a willow basket over her arm, opened Old Misery Guts' garden gate, walked up the garden path and knocked on the front door. Her rosy cheeked face looked like she smiled a lot, and her grey hair was tied up neatly in a bun. It was one of those beautiful, blue skied sunny days with not a breath of wind, where, if you went to the top of Blackford Hill, you could see clearly the city of Edinburgh laid out in all its glory, way out to sea and over to Fife.

Grumpily, Old Misery Guts, who was about to have a nice cup of tea out of her favourite cup, went to answer the door and was about to say, "Away ye go old pedlar woman!" when the old woman with a big cheery smile on her face said,

"Oh I'm no' selling anything. I was just passing and had to stop and tell you, what a very fine apple tree you have – it must have the best, most rosy, most delicious apples in all of Scotland." Looking round she added, "What a well-kept garden as well. You must be so proud."

Now this went down very well with Old Misery Guts, for she was indeed very proud of her garden and especially her apple tree. The woman continued,

"Do you think I could maybe have one or two to give a sweet taste in my mouth, on my journey?" Well Grumpy Guts had never been asked so nicely, nor praised so fulsomely and she surprised herself by saying,

"Och aye, you can have some, go and help yourself." So the old woman did so, filling her basket up with rosy red apples. She came back and said,

"For your kindness I will give you one wish – for anything at all."

Now I don't know what you would wish for if you were granted such a wish – a fabulous house with servants, become younger, have no aches and pains? But all Grumpy Guts could think of was to stop all the apple thieves for once and all.

"I wish that anyone who touches my apple tree will stick to it and not be able to become unstuck unless I tell them they are free."

"Your wish shall be granted." said the old woman, "Just say, 'Stuck to the apple tree you will be, till you promise never to steal from me!'"

The next day three little laddies got to the garden wall and saw the juicy delicious apple branch hanging over it. The smallest laddie was punted up onto the wall. He got on tiptoe and reached up to pick the nearest apple and his hand got stuck. It would not come off no matter how hard he pulled or shook it. Old Misery Guts came out shouting

"That'll teach ye - ye wee tyke! You can stay there for a bit and I might just free you later if you promise never to steal my apples again. Later she came back and said, "Stuck to the apple tree you will be, till you promise never to steal from me!" The boy tearfully nodded and said,

"Naw I'll no' steal yer rotten apples again! I'm telling ma mammy on you missus!!"

"You just do that!" Old Misery Guts shouted, as the wee laddie sped off, wiping his runny nose down his sleeve.

Then Auld Hamish came hirpling along the road. The smell of the apples and the way they almost shone on the tree, rosy and red, tempted him as usual. He balanced on his good leg and stretched up with his walking stick to knock the nearest apple down. But his stick stuck to the apple and his hand stuck to the stick and he couldn't get free. Misery Guts came out and said,

"That'll teach you to go scrumping at your age! Stuck to the apple tree you will be, until you promise never to steal from me!"

"I willnae dae it again missus," Hamish replied. "Honest, take your spell offa me, ma hurdies is loupin! "

So Hamish was freed and went hirpling down the path, muttering under his breath.

Then one day a very tall, thin stranger dressed in a midnight black hooded cloak with a scythe in his hand came to Old Misery Gut's door.

"I dinnae need anything scythed. Go away!" she said. She thought the man had a very odd appearance, especially with that ancient looking scythe. When she tried to see his face, she could see only darkness. A ripple of fear ran through her thin body, and she pulled her shawl around her shoulders.

"What do you want?" she said. In a deep, dark voice he replied,

"I am Death and I have come for you."

Now normally when Death said that people ran away screaming, but this old lady said,

"O aye, if you give me a minute I'll go and get ready. Why don't you pick one of my juicy, delicious apples while you are waiting?"

Well Death was amazed – no-one had ever offered him something before, so he put his scythe against the wall, then stretching up on his long boney, skeletal toes, he reached his boney, skeletal fingers up to get the biggest, shiniest apple he could see and was immediately stuck fast. No matter how much he pulled and jiggled and joogled and shoogled, he could not free himself.

"There you shall stay!" said the old woman smiling to herself at outwitting Death, as she went inside and sat down to eat the egg she had boiled for breakfast. But when she tried to crack the egg with her knife, it would not break, no matter how hard she tried. That's odd, she thought and went to get the fire lit, to put the kettle on for tea. But the wood would not burn. "I'll go down to the butchers and get some bacon for breakfast" she thought.

But when she came to the middle of Blackford village, the butcher was chasing a pig down the street with a cleaver.

"Any bacon?" asked the woman.

"NO!" exclaimed the butcher "No bacon today, the pig will not die, for every time I kill it, back to life it comes! Nothing seems to die today!"

"Oh dear, it's my fault because I have stopped Death from doing its job and nothing is dying. I will have to go back and free him."

So she returned home and there was Death still stuck to the apple tree.

"Well Death" she said "I'd better set you free. The world is in chaos when you do not do your job."

"Thank you," said Death. "It was getting uncomfortable stuck there. Since you did free me I shall not come for you yet. Goodbye!" and off he went with his scythe in his hand.

And do you know I'm not sure if he ever came back for the old woman – maybe she is alive even to this day!

JOHN QURESHI

John lives in Edinburgh and has lived between there in Glasgow all his life. In spite of this, he has international connections being Pakistani on his father's side and married to an Italian. He feels these connections provide with him a wealth of material to draw upon for storytelling. In spite, or perhaps because, of his serious job, he loves the escapism, spontaneity and performative silliness that storytelling brings. In doing so, he draws upon his previous university studies in English Literature, Theatre Studies and Primary Education, alongside his enjoyment of regaling younger relatives with wacky tales. He likes stories from the past and present but also likes to bring in different popular culture references where he can.

I FEEL HUNGRY

John Qureshi

*This story is inspired by the poem 'Goody Blake and Harry Gill' by
William Wordsworth, which he published in his iconic book of poetry
'Lyrical Ballads', co-written with Samuel Taylor Coleridge. Wordsworth
himself was thought to have taken inspiration for this tale from local
folklore from the Lake District area, as indeed he did with many other of
his poems. I have set my story in twenty-first century Edinburgh with
other key differences, including the ending but I think the poem does still
have resonance today.*

*So, our story starts in a manner in which the other stories you hear today
are unlikely to begin…*

Ben fell asleep in front of the Playstation.

He had been carrying out back-to-back all-nighters, fuelled
by black coffee, fast-food and screen time, in order to catch out
the little Neds who had been going through his bins. He was
sitting in a comfortable living room in a suburban part of
Edinburgh, in a nicer house than many of his contemporaries
were able to afford. He sat surrounded with his high-definition
TV, with surround sound and access to various Sky Sports
channels, Netflix, the latest games consoles, a top of the range
aquarium and a pile-up of take away boxes and empty cans of
craft lager. He was single with a well-paid job and no real
responsibilities or dependants.

Yet in the midst of this 'idyll' there was a fly in the ointment.
One that was getting bigger and more irritating. He had been in
his new home for a few months when he noticed that the take-
aways and left-over food he heaped by the bins from various
parties had been unwrapped, with the packets scattered round.
Originally, he had assumed this was due to foxes and put out

trail cameras. But these showed a person not wildlife. A person wearing a hood. Full of self-righteous outrage, he began to leave half-empty pizza boxes outside as bait. He intended to catch the miscreant and call the police.

As the weeks passed and he still had not caught whoever it was, what had started as nagging annoyance turned into obsession. If kids from the local estate were coming by and causing trouble this kind of thing needed to be nipped in the bud. He visualised gangs of them slowly taking over the neighbourhood. Ben had worked hard to live in an area like this. And now a swarm of little maggots had come to ruin things. If his neighbours didn't take this as seriously as he did then he would just have to roll up his sleeves and 'bang some skulls together' himself.

He had been pulling a few of these all-night vigils now and his senior management had started to comment on his ragged appearance, the bags under his eyes and the impact on his previous high-flying performance at work. It was too late to step back from his self-appointed 'mission' now, but the sooner the matter was dealt with, satisfactorily and decisively, the better.

All of a sudden, he was roused by a noise. The alarm he had set inside the pizza box! Finally, his plan had paid off! He rushed out and saw the hooded figure! At last! They weren't going to get away this time! They were going to pay for the misery of the last few weeks! No escape for this waster who had caused a hard-working tax-payer like Ben all this trouble and stress now! Angrily, he grabbed an arm and shook them, all the while trying to remember at the back of his head his original rational plan to call the police.

"Just what do you think you're doing?" No answer. He shook them harder, his voice getting louder,

"Just what the Hell do you think you've been doing going through my bins?"

He couldn't stop himself. For how long he wasn't quite sure, maybe for ten seconds, a minute, he let the frustration and rage and tiredness of the last couple of weeks take over. The words that flew out of him came back in a blur: "Waster!"; "Low life scum"; "Never had a job"; "Scrounging off decent people"; "Honestly, people like you don't deserve to live."

He stopped when he saw the person he had apprehended had gone limp with shock and the hood fell back. It was a middle-aged woman, who appeared to have frozen with fear. He stepped back, letting go of her arm.

Fortunately, at that point, common sense and compassion kicked in. Instead of calling for a police car, Ben summoned an ambulance and after a few tersely answered questions, the woman was whisked away.

"Well, that was unfortunate," Ben thought to himself. "I hadn't meant for that to happen. Then again, if you sneak around raking through folks' bins at night, what do you expect?"

He felt strangely peckish then. He went into his kitchen to sort himself out with a plate of chips. He couldn't wait for them and rummaged through his cupboards while they cooked. Once they were ready, he ate them up far more quickly than he expected. Still hungry and raking through the jars of food in the house, he found himself ordering a take-away. He ended up sleeping in, sneaking in to work the following morning half-way through an important meeting. His late-coming did not go unnoticed.

In the following weeks and months at work, various 'constructive interventions' proved to be of no avail. All Ben could think of was eating. Weeks of poor performance appraisals, missed appointments and targets, were put down to drugs and alcohol. Ben's managers, previously so impressed by the early impact he had made, could not accept at face value the explanation he provided. Eventually they let him go. It was a regrettable decision, but what else could be expected? Business was business and they could not afford to have passengers no matter how impressive they might have been in the past. And the only explanation he would provide which, of course, was no explanation at all, was that he felt hungry.

People tried to help but to no avail. No matter what help was offered he kept saying, "I feel hungry". Eventually friends and family drifted away, after various broken promises, let downs, tears and frustrations. He could only repeat, "I feel hungry."

Social Services stepped in, thinking the reasons for the loss of his job, house, friends and family, the shopliftings and bin-rummagings, were all down to substance abuse. They were mistaken and Ben's hunger could not be satisfied.

One day out on the street during the Christmas period, two years on from the initial skirmish around his bins, he encountered a woman out and about with her family enjoying the festive entertainments. He was ravenously attacking a very large bucket of fried chicken, so they were startled by his declaration that he felt hungry and his request for money to buy something to eat.

The children were pleading for a go in the ice-rink and their mother accompanied them. Ben was surprised when she returned a few minutes later with a burger.

"I can't believe you came back. Hardly anyone does," he said.

"You remind me of someone I knew not so long ago," she responded.

She went on to recount her own recent past. How, in spite of working as a nurse at the local hospital, she had been struggling to raise her kids on a single income. This was exacerbated by various past financial decisions, debts and loans to pay for Christmas. She often went hungry to feed her children and so on her way back from night shifts, she found herself going through bins to feed herself. She could not get enough to eat. Until one night she was caught. She looked at Ben pointedly.

Yet after being caught out, things began to improve for her. Colleagues she had previously hidden her problems from began to understand. Help and advice was offered, and she was able to pay off debts. Things improved. She met her new partner. And two years on, here she was.

As soon as she began to relate her tale, Ben realised who she was. Shame for his past actions overwhelmed him,

"I am the one who set the traps to catch you going through my food waste," he admitted. "I am the one who shook you. I am the one who yelled at you. It's alright, I don't need food from you".

"I know who you are," the woman reassured him, handing over the food. "But now you are hungry, and it is time for you to eat."

He took the burger and placing it in his mouth began to chew. He swallowed his first mouthful. For the first time in two years, Ben felt full.

ELAINE ROBERTSON

Elaine has lived in Midlothian just outside Edinburgh city most of her life. After a career in libraries where her greatest love was to share stories with the children from nurseries, schools, and the local community, she moved into the profession of oral storytelling through The Storytelling Centre. She has been expanding her repertoire of stories telling in festivals and local community events and has been telling to zoom storytelling groups all over the country during lockdown with stories gleaned from all over the world, but especially her own local community. Elaine also sings with a local choir and in care homes.

CAMP MEG

Elaine Robertson

Recently I have been working with a heritage community project to keep local Midlothian stories alive. I was attracted to this story drawn from the collection by J.C. Carrick in his book Around Dalkeith and Camp Meg.

Margaret Hawthorn was running for her life. She had travelled far from her home in Galloway. She found herself in Newbattle, Midlothian, on the post road at The Old Sun Inn, a place for travellers to stop and rest on a long journey. It exists to this day but now it is a private dwelling which still has the insignia of the sun carved into the stone at the front. There was to be no rest for Margaret on this day, however, and she needed to find a place of safety. How had she come to this point? It seemed not too long ago she had a grand house, land, a husband, and a beautiful young son.

All that had changed with the early unexpected death of her husband. She lived in a time when men could claim the land from widows if they could prove they had more right to it. She was hounded by a neighbouring farmer who claimed the land was promised to him. He pursued her relentlessly till she snapped and shot him with her husband's gun. When she saw the blood oozing from his body, she knew she had to flee or she would hang! No one would believe she had only been trying to defend her property.

Leaving her beloved son with good friends she disguised herself as a man, cutting off her long hair, putting on a long coat and pulling a hat down over her face. She jumped on her horse and rode for her life.

She hoped that the isolation she needed was at the top of the hill at nearby D'Arcy. As luck would have it there was a beacon house there which had been used as a vantage point to spot Napoleon's ships coming into the Forth, now abandoned and fallen into disrepair.

She was able to set up a sparse home. She planted vegetables, caught wild rabbits to skin and eat and collected water from the burn. The farmer was impressed with her self-sufficiency and being in need of a farm hand he offered her a job not caring that she was a woman.

She proved to have an instinctive knowledge of animals and came to be considered a 'horse whisperer' who used herbs and potions on sick livestock. Her innovative procedure of suspending a lame horse giving the leg time to heal instead of having to shoot the animal meant that other farmers and landowners would bring sick animals to her to cure. The deal was if she couldn't cure them, she could shoot them and eat them, a practical arrangement that suited everyone concerned.

Because of her strange appearance the local rumour had it that she must be a witch, and it was lucky for her that the time of the witch finders was at an end. Some young lads thought it would be good sport to push pennies under her door. That was fun for them until Meg, as she had become known, ran her sickle under the door saying,

"Mind I don't accidentally chop off your fingers now!"

They certainly had more respect for her after that! She didn't mind the boys and told them stories about seeing the devil roaming the fields as they sat outside around a fire. She preferred to be outdoors since her dwelling was spartan, tree stumps for chairs, her bed consisted of long thick tree branches covered with bracken, rough blankets she had found in the house, cloth stuffed with sheep's wool for a pillow.

No one knew her story except the farmer, and she was known as Camp Meg because the area was an old Roman Camp. As she grew more confident that she was safe she started to join the horse racing at nearby Musselburgh. She won most of the time which annoyed the men, but the organisers decided that she won fair and square. She used the prize money for her beloved drink and baccy for she loved to drink and smoke with the men. She was not bothered by male advances because she smelt of animals and was never too clean!

Far from her respectable beginnings she was no longer fussy about appearances. One time some of the local boys made her a soup. They used a headless chicken, still with the feathers on and vegetables straight from the fields, neither washed nor peeled. She exclaimed it was the best soup she had ever tasted.

One day there was a knock on her door and a handsome young man stood there asking for Margaret Hawthorne. At first hostile and thinking to set her fierce dog on him she found out he was looking for his mother. She scanned his face and saw the features of her dead husband there.

"I am your mother," she said falling to the floor in a faint. He spent three precious days with her and tried to persuade her to return to Galloway, but she explained that there was no life for her there. She loved the freedom of her life on the farm. This was the last time she would see her son.

There is a superstition that a fierce hurricane blowing marks the passage of a witch's spirit into the unseen. The night before Meg died there was just such a storm. It was so bad that the roads and hedges were covered, and no one was able to get to the camp except for her friend the farmer. He worried for her as he climbed the hill despite the snow and found her on her doorstep blanketed in snow, face up looking at the open sky.

Dead.

HARRIET GRINDLEY

Another founder member of the Blatherers, with fond memories of those early meetings upstairs at the Waverley. Born in Brighton, raised in London, Harriet likes a good song and a good story, and even more when the two are put together! She left London at seventeen seeking family roots in Fife and never went back. Education has ranged from Mediaeval History at St Andrews University, Human Resource Management in Glasgow and latterly Gaelic at Sabhal Mòr Ostaig on Skye, employment has taken her from financial services to shop keeper and acupuncturist but the stories, song and welcome in Scotland have never varied.

THREE WITCHES OF KINTAIL

Harriet Grindley

This is one of the first stories I heard told in Edinburgh's very own Guid Crack Club upstairs in the then very rackety surroundings of the Waverley Bar. It's a traditional story told in many versions throughout Scotland in both English and Gaelic. I love the fun our witches are clearly having. Often, they go to London, but this time I thought a little jaunt to Edinburgh might hit the spot! And, of course, I can't resist pairing a story with a good song ...

Rann
Thèid mi dhachaigh hi ro dhachaigh,
Thèid mi dhachaigh chrò Chin t-Sàile,
Thèid mi dhachaigh ho ro dhachaigh,
Thèid mi dhachaigh chrò Chinn t-Sàile

Seist
Thèid mi fhìn, leam fhìn, leam fhìn ann,
Thèid mi fhìn, leam fhìn à Geàrrloch,
Thèid mi fhìn, leam fhìn, leam fhìn ann
'S gabhaidh mi 'n rathad mòr Chrò Chinn t-Sàile.

Verse
I will go home hi ro homewards
I will go home to the byre at Kintail
I will go home ho ro homewards
I will go home to the byre at Kintail

Chorus
Alone I will go, I'll take myself there
I'll go there myself, alone from Gairloch.

Alone I will go, I'll take myself there
I'll take the high road to the byre at Kintail.

Beneath five mountains, the Sisters of Kintail, Donald worked his small croft in Invershiel, where he kept cows or *cròdh*. No self-respecting highlander would be without cattle, but it was the sea that was his joy. Every fine day he would take his small boat out following the sea roads west to Skye, north to Applecross, Gairloch and beyond. He knew every inlet, every channel, as you know the veins on the back of your hand.

But this fine day the black squall came out of a blue sky. The white horses began to trot, canter and gallop on the waves and his boat swayed and tossed in winds and lashing rain. When evening fell and the winds gentled to soft sighs, he found himself on a shore he did not know and his boat, well his boat was broken.

On the headland he saw a solitary cottage with one light glimmering. He poked his head over the window sill. Inside he spied three of the oldest women he had ever seen. One was so old that her chin came up to her nose, and one was so old that her nose came down to her chin, and one was *so* old she bent right over and her nose touched her toes. Could they possibly help him, he wondered?

He raised his hand but before he could knock a voice said,

"Come in Donald," and the door opened. The three crones appeared delighted.

"Come in, come away in, sit yourself down by the fire, get that wet coat from off you. We were hoping you would get here in time and us just about to have a bite to eat. We've the broth, and the oatcakes, and a tasty bit fish and will you help yourself now to all of it?"

They made a feast and what good craik they had! Soon Donald was telling his stories of the sea and how he had foundered the boat, and his hosts told tales of years gone by.

101

The meal came to its end and the women began to speak to each other.

"What an evening, with just the right sort of young man, it's been too long, don't you think?" And another said,

"Yes surely, just a little one would make no harm? Him such a braw, bold, bonny one."

They looked to their eldest sister, the one whose nose touched her very toes, and it seemed she agreed, because she got up. She took a stool, with a couple of boards to boost her while her sisters held her steady, to reach high, high into the shadows of the rafters. Donald saw there, on a shelf, a dusty bottle, glasses and two cloth caps, one red, one green.

She handed round the glasses, pouring each a full measure. Then she put the green cap on her head, raised the whisky to her lips and cried,

"*Thalla dhan bhaile mhòr!* Away to the big city!" Shluurrp, she drained the glass and Shwooop, in an instant she was gone. Just the green cap left on her chair.

The second sister picked up the cap and lifted her glass.

"*Thalla dhan bhaile!* Off to the city!" Shlurp, and Shwoop, and only the cap on the chair. And now the third sister the very same thing: Cap; glass; "Off to the city!" Gone!

Donald was alone in the cottage, a full dram before him and the cap on the chair beside him. What to do? He sniffed the whisky and picked up the cap, he looked at it from every side, but in the end, with the cap on his head, he picked up the glass and took the smallest sip.

"Off to the city," he said cautiously, and with a Schwooo and a Whoop, he felt the whistling of air in his bones and there he was!

In Edinburgh. In the Royal Mile. Just outside John Knox' house right where the Storytelling Centre is today. In front of him were three sisters, three pretty sisters: one with the sweetest dimpled chin, one with a nose pert as an apple and one tall and slender as a willow wand.

"What took you so long Donald?" she asked, clearing a frog of age from her throat. Then she linked her arm in his and they began to explore.

Up and down the High Street they went, exclaiming at magic shows and fortune tellers. They examined the gloves and trinkets in the luckenbooths, and the savoury morsels from the street braziers. The sisters were checking the fashions.

"Look how short skirts are this year!" they exclaimed. "And those boots, and that muffler! We could make something just as fine at home don't you think?"

Even Donald caught himself admiring a pair of canary yellow stockinged breeches. Up and down they went, they looked over the Mound and saw the works draining the great loch in the middle of Princes Street and the spread of New Town going up beyond

"Hasn't it all changed since last time?" they asked. Afternoon grew on to evening and they looked at each other.

"Is it time?" "No, no! the night is young, there's the new Assembly Rooms in George Street." "Shall we not go and join the dancing there?"

They hailed a passing carriage and the coachman dropped them off, tallest sister waving a purse. Donald helped each sister out and admired their most exquisite ball gowns. Indeed, he himself had the swing of a fine kilt at his knee with a lawn shirt upon his back.

"He's with us," the girls said airily to the doormen, "he's our escort." And they sailed into the splendid new rooms, tall arched windows ablaze with glittering chandeliers. Into the dancing they went. There were country dances, reels, strathspeys. Donald even dared some waltzes and of course he was never short of the prettiest of partners.

Arm in arm they went down to the supper rooms, where such a spread was laid! They tasted everything! Twice! At last, the tallest sister whispered a word to a footman and shortly a serving boy crossed the room solemnly bearing four small glasses of amber liquid on a sliver salver.

From a pocket tallest sister brought out a red cap and picked up one of the glasses.

"*Thèid mi dhachaigh*, Back to Kintail." she cried, knocking back the dram. Shlurp! Just as before, Schwooop! She was gone with only the red cap left behind. The second sister took the cap.

"*Thèid mi dhachaigh!* I will go home!" and she was gone. Third sister; cap, dram.

"Back to Kintail! Shlurp! Schwoop!

But, as Donald put his fingers out to the cap on the chair, the Master of Ceremonies crossed the room with measured tread and put a hand heavy on his shoulder

"You have questions to answer, scoundrel! You have been impersonating a Highland Chieftain, you and your accomplices, and have swindled a trail from High Street booths, town coachmen, countless hostelries and our own subscription for the dance and supper. All appear to have been paid, not with coin, but with silver buttons."

Donald spent the night in the Tollbooth cells, the bells of St Giles counting out the hours. In the morning he was up before the Judge in Chambers Street. Justice in those days was harsh and swift. The Judge put on his Black cap.

"For crimes of passing false currency and of impersonating a Chieftain to inveigle yourself and your accomplices into good society and there purloining four fine suppers and ancillary refreshments, you are sentenced to death and you shall be hanged in the Grassmarket this very afternoon."

And so, from Chambers Street down Candlemaker Row to the Grassmarket where a great crowd was gathered. The scaffold was set up opposite 'The Last Drop' and Donald was set to mount the platform. This was a lot worse than a hole in the boat. But wait!

"I've a last request, haven't I?"

"You have," grudged the Constable.

"Well, I've a last request and this is it. I'd like to die wearing my own red cap and with the taste of my own highland whisky on my lips. You'll find the cap in my back pocket, and surely that pub over there can part with a nip? A double forbye!'

"It'll be a single," muttered the Constable, "and no fancy malt mind. Make it quick!"

And indeed, he did make it quick. No sooner had Donald the cap on his head than he leant forward to taste the whisky and whispered,

"*Thèid mi dhachaigh!* Home to Kintail!"

Shlurp. Schwoop. Air whistled through his body.

He found himself back on the beach beside his broken boat, and right there, around his neck, was just the piece of rope he needed to make the repairs.

JACK MARTIN

Jack has lived in Edinburgh his whole life. He became a storyteller after a lifetime as an entertainer, doing pantomime for sixteen years and stand-up comedy on stage and in bars. For thirty-five years he worked full-time as a joinery instructor in a Rehab Team providing support to psychiatric patients in the Royal Edinburgh Hospital. All Jack's stories come from his imagination, often humorous and set in his own home town.

WEE GEORDIE MCCLORY

Jack Martin

I like to write stories about places I know. This story conjures up life in Edinburgh in the 1940s and 1950s, the heyday of the city's iconic department store, Jenners, where this fantastical tale of a young boy's experiment with invisibility takes place. Read on.

Wee Geordie was an only child, his father was a soldier and spent most of his time abroad. Wee Geordie clung to his mother. They went everywhere together. His mother loved to visit Jenners, a large department store at the east end of Princes Street, with very little money to spend. She would wander from one floor to another, dreaming of what she would buy if only she had the money. A soldier's pay was rather low. There was only just enough money to feed herself and wee Geordie. He was always pointing out lovely clothes and shoes to her and promising what he would buy her when he was big! "If only" she would think.

One day, their wanderings in the store took them to the top floor. Wee Geordie saw a door at the far end on which was a large sign, *Ladies Changing Room*. Wee Geordie was puzzled,

"Mummy, what are they changing into?"

His mother was feeling rather tired. It had been a long walk through the many floors and not being her usual kind self she snapped at him,

"Monkeys!"

Wee Geordie was shocked. He rather liked monkeys. On his one and only visit to the Edinburgh Zoological Gardens, out of the many animals on view, he found the monkeys the most interesting. On reflection, many of the old ladies he knew did look a bit like monkeys, but he could never see them climbing trees!

That night he went through his father's large collection of books, with no luck about ladies changing into monkeys. However, there was a rather strange book, all about old customs and beliefs of the East. It was far too complicated for Geordie, but there was one chapter that explained how to become invisible with a list of ingredients to use! One item he spotted was *horse urine*. He asked the old milkman, who had a horse, what *horse urine* was. The old man laughed and said,

"It means horse pee."

Geordie got a jar full. Along with a few bits and pieces he got from the rubbish bin, now he was all set.

The next day, sitting in front of his mother's dressing mirror, he took a sip of the horse pee mixture, and nothing happened! Or so he thought: but looking closer in the mirror, there was no sign of his hands or head, just his shirt and jersey! Then, while he was looking in the mirror, the One O'Clock Gun went off with a bang, and once more Geordie was returned to visibility! Now he had the solution to re-visibility as well: a good loud noise.

The next day, Geordie made his way to Jenners, clutching his jar of horse pee mixture. Before he drank the mixture, he took off all his clothes and left them in a bag beside a large rubbish bin while he went up to the *Ladies Changing Room* to see the monkeys. Alas, he was disappointed. When he got to the room there were no monkeys, just ladies changing the clothes they had on. One lady dropped her purse. Geordie picked it up and offered it back to her, forgetting he was invisible. All the lady saw was her purse in mid-air coming towards her. She screamed so loud that Geordie lost his invisibility and was left completely naked. Turning quickly, he ran downstairs to get his clothes, but someone had found them and taken them away.

Geordie had to make his way home with not a stitch on. Luckily it was a warm day and Princes Street Gardens has lots of bushes!

110

MARIA MACDONELL

Maria has lived in Edinburgh many times. She comes and goes and always returns. For about forty years she has enjoyed many adventures in the creative and performing arts as an actor, writer, television presenter, storyteller, and facilitator. Her escapades go on, so long as she does.

(Maria's name is pronounced Mar-eye-yah)

WHEN LOCH FLEW AWAY

Maria MacDonell

This story is inspired by an old European folk tale and by my experience of Covid-19 Lockdown in a beautiful Angus glen in north east Scotland.

There was once a happy loch. She was happy with the hills which held her in their wide arms. She was happy with the sun which warmed her and the rain which filled her. She was happy with the wind which tickled her surface making her ripple all over, sending little frothy waves out to her pebbly shores. She was happy caring for all the fish and frogs and newts and toads that lived within her and she was happy welcoming all the otters and ducks and swans who came to her for food. And she was especially happy with Heron who stood very still beside her, on a rock, and whispered ghost stories to her through the night.

She was happy. Until the people came.

They had been kept indoors for months and they were so excited, laughing and swimming and splashing and playing and Loch was happy with that.

But she was not happy with the cars and trucks and motorbikes which they left higgledy-piggeldy, hugger-mugger, what-the-heck, and all around her. She was not happy with their inflatable furniture and their plastic tubs and wrappings and their throwaway barbeques.

She was not happy that when they left in their vehicles, in a cloud of exhaust, they left all the rest of it behind.

The plastic entangled itself in the trees so birds could not nest, the throwaway barbeques scorched the grass and cut the soft toes of the otters, plastic choked the fish and broken glass lay amongst the pebbles grazing the bellies of ducks who sat there in the sun.

112

The people tormented Loch and they were tormented too. They were arguing and complaining and worrying and never getting enough of what they wanted and never stopping still to look and listen and understand. And in time they became ill and sad.

And the loch, dressed up in all that junk? Well, she didn't recognise herself.

The hills closed their eyes in shame. What could they have done? The sun hid behind a cloud. The wind whistled a merry tune to keep its mind off nasty things. And Heron? She considered her position. Then she lifted her long grey wings and reluctantly she flew away to find better company.

Loch saw her go. She understood. She sighed.

And then she did a remarkable thing. She gathered all her strength. She gathered herself together.

And then Loch too flew away. Yes.

Over the hills where Deer and Fox and Hare looked up in complete astonishment. Over the forests where Pine Martin and Squirrel quarrelled about who saw her first. Over the fields where Mouse and Stoat raced to keep up with her and on through the blue sky with Eagle flying alongside - a beautiful shimmering loch gliding through the clear air, holding to her heart all the fish and frogs and toads and newts that lived within her so that not a single creature should drop.

Until she came to a glen of gentle heathery slopes and sun dappled woods and there she let herself down gently, until with a gasp…Aaaaaah… she came to rest, sending little frothy waves out across the land. And there she stayed.

And the people? Well, they came back. They were sorry. They came peacefully on foot and they left no litter. They came in respect of the wondrous grace and beauty of Loch.

And do you know? Then those people flourished.

FINALE

The Parting Glass

"Thank you so much, Maria. A timely and cautionary tale that had me turn greener with every passing sentence. Yet I am neither envious nor inclined to vomit. Nah, I just want to save the planet. But before that, let's wind this thing up.

And you know in some ways, I feel that we have almost turned full circle and I am reminded of Franziska and the very first story of the evening. About storytellers and their propensity to retell or refashion the stories that they have heard and loved while adding their own special twist. And we have had a lot of that tonight and hopefully we have been educated, cheered and given some food for thought as we prepare to take our leave of each other. I hope we will leave with our love of stories refreshed and renewed and determined to retell some of the stories that have captured our imaginations.

By my way of thinking a beautiful story is like a beautiful, scrumptious, calorific laden cake, smiling seductively at us from the patisserie's window; neither of them fulfils their potential till they are taken down and shared. But there is a subtle difference.

We have all grown up very well-aware that we cannot have our cake and eat it and neither choice is ideal. A story, on the other hand, is quite different. True, it isn't quite a story until it is retold and shared but far from losing anything in the telling, and our own special twisting, it will be enhanced and, unlike the cake, we can go back to it again and again. Please do try it.

And so, as we prepare to set out on our journeys to that spot of the Burgh or Beyond that we call home all that is left for me is to thank you for coming and staying with us, to ask you to come again and to invite you to join with us in singing the travelling folk's favourite farewell, 'The Parting Glass'.

114

Oh kind friends and companions
Come join me in rhyme
And lift up your voices in chorus wi' mine
Let's drink and be merry
All grief to refrain
For we may or might never
All meet here again.

So here's a health to the company
May it not be our last
Let's drink and be merry
All out of one glass
Let's drink and be merry
All grief to refrain
For we may or might never
All meet here again

O my ship lies in harbour
She is ready to sail
God grant her safe voyage
Without any gale
And if we should meet again
By Land or by sea
I will always remember
Your Kindness to me

So here's a health to the company
May it not be our last
Let's drink and be merry
All out of one glass
Let's drink and be merry
All grief to refrain
For we may or might never
All meet here again"

That's it. All done. Time to go. Come on. Coat on. To the door. Step outside.

It's hard to part.

Darkness has come. Let's stand and look a while into the soft velvet sky. Street lights are glowing. The city has changed.

It is a little cold. Tie your scarf. Pull on your hat. Let's stand and feel the drizzle on our cheeks.

It's hard to part.

We've been to many places. We've seen many things. We've met many people. We've journeyed far.

Let's stand together a while in the street.

Thank you for coming.

Let's do this again.

Printed in Great Britain
by Amazon

86116936R00073